CUFFED BY A Gangsta

LA & Mocha

A NOVEL BY
TESHERA C

© *2019 Royalty Publishing House*

Published by Royalty Publishing House
www.royaltypublishinghouse.com

ALL RIGHTS RESERVED
Any unauthorized reprint or use of the material is prohibited. No part of this book may be reproduced or transmitted in any form or by any means, electronic or mechanical, including photocopying, recording, or by any information storage without express permission by the author or publisher. This is an original work of fiction. Names, characters, places and incidents are either products of the author's imagination or are used fictitiously and any resemblance to actual persons, living or dead, is entirely coincidental.
Contains explicit language & adult themes suitable for ages 16+ only.

Royalty Publishing House is now accepting manuscripts from aspiring or experienced urban romance authors!

WHAT MAY PLACE YOU ABOVE THE REST:

Heroes who are the ultimate book bae: strong-willed, maybe a little rough around the edges but willing to risk it all for the woman he loves.

Heroines who are the ultimate match: the girl next door type, not perfect - has her faults but is still a decent person. One who is willing to risk it all for the man she loves.

The rest is up to you! Just be creative, think out of the box, keep it sexy and intriguing!

If you'd like to join the Royal family, send us the first 15K words (60 pages) of your completed manuscript to submissions@royaltypublishing-house.com

SYNOPSIS

"When are you going to learn that it never ends? You take one of theirs, they take one of yours and the mess just keeps going."

When two people from the opposite sides of the track come together, is it fate or would you call it just a chance encounter that should've been left at just that, an encounter? Philly is known for its infamous gangs, but no gang is as deadly or lethal as the Notorious Hitta' gang. With the untimely death of NHG leader Sco, LA, next in line is forced into a position that he at one point wanted nothing to do with. LA is a hot head who graduated from the school of hard knocks and bleeds NHG. Now with LA leading the crew, he vows to avenge his brother's death, but his tunnel vision is thrown off when Mocha Hart comes into his life.

Mocha, a promising Pediatric nurse, and a boss chick wants nothing more than to put her heart ache from previous relationships aside to focus on her career. Mocha and LA couldn't be more different and while Mocha has a M.S. at the end of her name, LA has NHG before his and in his eyes, nothing comes before the gang. A chance encounter connects the two, but

TESHERA C.

Mocha soon learns that she is connected to NHG's rival gang, The Natural Born Killers, more than she knows. When Mocha's loyalty is tested, she must decide if it's worth being a banger's girl or if fate made a mistake.

ASHLYN IS JUST TRYING to piece her life back together after losing her child's father and having to ultimately raise her child alone. After licking her wounds and being over men who toy with her heart, Ashlyn sets her sights on an old friend, who runs with NHG. When Ashlyn's new found relationship ends more quickly than it began, she questions her worth and if she even deserves to be loved.

PEACHES AND PISCES both want things that they cannot have, but they can't see past their own selfish wants to realize that we seldomly win when playing dirty. The women both long after NHG's infamous LA but must rethink their thirst trap plans when Mocha comes into the picture. Both envious of Mocha and willing to stop at nothing to get to LA, someone will win, and someone could end up getting burned.

IN THIS TALE of feuding rivals, love burns, and scandals, what will be more important; protecting the ones you love or claiming king of the streets?

What the fuck do you know?
   You don't even keep your nails clean.

— JUSTICE (POETIC JUSTICE)

ACKNOWLEDGMENTS

Here I am on my fourth book and it all still feels so surreal to me, but it has all been possible, thanks to my Royalty team. Thank you Porscha and Michelle for the hard work that you put in and helping to mold me into a better writer. To Shantel & Jaleesa: whew chile! Those countless nights of editing were hard, but we did it, so thank you. And lastly, my Bumble-Tee's; my sister in-law, baby cousin Tracy told me that y'all are the bomb and when my pen hits the paper, my goal is to write a banger for y'all. Thank you for the continuous support! The best is yet to come. Be great!

*To the Leary Family, I send my deepest condolences.
RIP DaDa!*

PROLOGUE

A lone tear slid down my eyes as I reminisced times with my boy CJ. CJ and I had grown up together in the mean streets of Philly and my mom took him in after his mom died, so we were more like brothers. I sat on the first row of the pews as my mom wept on my shoulders and the whole hood plied into the church; you would have thought a celebrity had died or something. Shit, I guess you could say CJ was a celebrity in his own right by the slew of the girls who attended the funeral claiming to be his main bitch. CJ and his player ways took my mind off his death for a moment.

This nigga stayed giving girls my number instead of his own. Bitches would be blowing me up left and right looking for his ass, and get mad when it was me, that was my boy though. CJ, my brother Sco, and I were as thick as thieves. No one could tell us shit, but that all changed the day CJ was killed. I remember him telling me to come to the party with him and turning him down because of school. Yeah, I was the one with the brains, a little nerdy some would say. Big booty Rudy was having a party at her house on a Thursday because her parents had gone out of town. Long story short, my mans got into it with some niggas from the west side and they shot him. My nigga laid out in the street for an hour, that is how long it took the paramedics to get to him.

TESHERA C.

My big brother Sco was now at the podium making everyone laugh, telling old ass jokes about CJ. He went on and on about CJ and his pretty boy ways along with his gift of gab when it came to the ladies. That nigga could charm the pants off anybody and their mama. Yeah, he had a few baby mamas too. I could hear him now, *"It's too many beautiful bitches in the world for me to just have one gang."* Sco and CJ were a part of the NHG, which is the Notorious Hitta' Gang. I tried to stay away from that stuff and left the gang shit to them. For real, the gang is what I believe killed my boy.

Everyone and their damn mama knew that NHG had been feuding with the Westside Gang, NBK, the Natural Born Killers, forever. My damn uncle had even died at the hands of the NBK, so I just didn't understand why Sco and CJ would want to live that life. I kept far away as possible from it and focused on school and shit; I just wasn't built for that type of stuff. I was the shortest in my junior class, standing at 5'3" and scrawny, with braces, acne, baby dreads, and whatever teenage problems one could think of. The only reason bitches even looked my way is because of Sco and CJ. Sco was the peanut colored brickhouse stallion and CJ was the Hershey colored pretty boy. The girls would fuck me just to get to them and I didn't mind if I was getting some pussy.

The funeral was coming to an end as we headed to the gravesite. My brother, a few more NHG guys, and myself served as the pallbearers as we lowered my boy into the ground. Man, there wasn't one dry eye in sight as my mother broke into song. Her voice sounded angelic though the was sadness in her heart was heard as well.

> We laughed at the darkness so scared that we lost it.
> we stood on the ceiling, you showed me love was all you
>   needed.
> Heaven couldn't wait for you,
> Heaven couldn't wait for you,
> Heaven couldn't wait for you, so gone on and go home.

Everyone was now boohooing just at the thought that CJ was never coming back, even Sco, who I had never seen cry in my seventeen years of living. Each word that my mom sang was true. She never treated CJ any differently from Sco and me, she actually treated him a tad bit better being that he didn't have any family. She would always say, "*CJ needs just a little bit more love than you boys. You have your mother and your father, and he has neither.* Those words replayed in my head as I stared at my weeping mother having to burry one of her sons.

I had to get ghost before I fucking lost it. The thought that I would never be able to laugh at one of CJ's corny jokes again haunted me. Ever since that day, I blamed myself; like why didn't I just go to the fucking party with him? I was one of the only ones who could calm his hot-tempered ass down when he was doing too much. I could've protected him that night. *Who am I kidding?* CJ protected me. In my eyes he and Sco were unbeatable, no one dared stepping to them. CJ and Sco were the same age, twenty, and even though I was years younger than them, they never left me out and were honestly my best friends.

I made my way to my beat-up Honda Civic, she didn't look good on the outside, but she got me from A to B. I drove with no destination in sight. Everyone would soon be meeting up at my house to eat and shit, but I wasn't feeling it. I needed to be alone honestly. I decided to stop at one of CJ's favorite spots, Ishkabibbles on South Street. There had been many arguments on who had the best cheesesteaks in Philly, but in my mind, it was not a debate. Ishkabibbles took the cake, no cap.

I entered and dapped my main man Raheem up. He owned the joint and always hooked CJ and me up with chicken phillys. I'd ordered my usual, chicken philly with salt, pepper, Provolone cheese, mayo, mustard, onions, light lettuce, and banana peppers, when I heard a familiar voice coming up behind me. I turned to see thick ass Tammi. I had wanted Tammi for years and she gave me no play, constantly saying that I was a lil' boy and some more shit.

"What's up Tammi?" I smirked.

"Hey, lil' LA," she said, before laughing. I didn't get it and I damn sure wasn't no lil LA,

even though I was pretty.

"Aye stop that shit Tammi. When you gone give a nigga some play?" I asked, seriously. Tammi was the type a girl that left nothing to the imagination. She pranced around in weave that damn near touched her ass in all kinds of skimpy ass dresses and she stayed teasing a nigga.

"Lance Anderson, you know that you are too young for me," she said, while cutting me in line.

"Age ain't shit, I will fuck you like a grown ass man," I said, confidently.

"See that's your problem right there. You sound like a lil' ass boy and I'm not into training. Tell yo' sexy ass brother Sco to holla though, that nigga is *oh my god* fine," she said, while dapping her friend up.

"Ain't he girl? I will suck the skin off his dick," the friend agreed.

All I could do was stare at the way her ass jumped in them leggings each time she got a lil' too excited thinking about my brother. Truth is, my brother definitely would fuck her, but that would be it. He had an old lady at home who he dipped out on from time to time, but she was everything to him and no fine big booty bitch could take that away. I still like Tammi though, her big glowing ass made me not think about CJ so much.

"Ummm, excuse me, can you go please? I'm not trying to be late to class while you're over there drooling over her."

I turned to see some blow-up looking chick with an arm full of books and glasses too big for her fucking face.

"Helloooo, you are holding up the line," she said, once more.

"Damn shorty chill. You shouldn't have stopped your ass here if you had to go to class anyway. You look like you could really lay off the subs anyway." I looked at all the shit she had in her hands. Ding dongs, skittles, chips, two Mr. Good bars, and a twister juice. Chubs knew damn well she needed a damn rice cake or something and not all that shit.

"Whatever," she said, while dropping her things on the counter and dashing out of the store. She really could use that jog.

I grabbed my sub from Raheem and spent the rest of the day chopping it up with him. I purposefully stayed there until all the people had gone home from my house. Yeah, coming to Iskabibbles was a little distraction from the shit I was going through, but once I got home the sad reality that my best friend was gone hit me all over again.

SCO

*M*y guys and I had been planning how we would retaliate against NBK for a few months now. I didn't know for sure, but I would bet my last dollar that they had something to do with the death of my brother. It had been three months since I had laid him to rest and I made a promise to him at his funeral that his death would not be in vain. Niggas thought that they could come into our territory and take one of ours without us taking a hundred of theirs, and they had us twisted. We had finally come up with a plan to raise some havoc. I was fucking one of the NBK's girlfriends and she was spilling everything about them. They lil' poe' ass meet up spots, where their mamas stayed, and some more shit. Tonight was the night that me and the gang would finally put our plans into effect. La La had let me know that some of them were gone be meeting up with a connect for some pills, so what I did was find out who that connect was and cancelled the meeting. They asses would be flabbergasted when they realized that instead of their connects meeting them it would be us

    I got my mind right as the mission would go down in about two hours. I sat on the bed in deep thought as my girl Ashlyn wobbled her big self into the room eating on something as usual. Ashlyn was eight months pregnant and big as a house, but still beautiful as ever. If anyone asked who Sco's girl was they would definitely say Ash. Yeah, I fucked around in the streets from time to time, but Ashlyn had my heart. No other female would ever come before her and if they tried blowing up my spot, I would kill their ass.

"What you in here thinking about?" Ashlyn asked, while stuffing her face with raw cookie dough.

"My seed that you're carrying, that's what I'm thinking about," I laughed and then pulled her into me. She started to pout, and I didn't know why.

"What's up Ash, why you looking like that?"

"Because, when she gets here, you're going to forget all about me. Everything will be about her," she said, while pointing to her stomach. Ash was so damn spoiled from her parents and now me. All I could do was laugh at her seriousness.

"Baby, of course I will have love for my baby girl, but that doesn't mean that there won't be any love for you. You and Ross will both be my number ones. Don't act like that."

"Okay," she said, before placing her fat, juicy lips on mine. I remember when my girl was a size two and now, she had to be a size eight or nine. I loved it though, actually I loved everything about Ashlyn. She was a freshman in college when I rolled up on her, she was sitting with her girls outside eating lunch. I straight threw that shit in the trash and told her to let me take her out for lunch. Mannn, she cursed my ass out, calling me all kinds of rude and belligerent ass holes. And she certainly did not go with me, so for the entire year I brought her lunch even though for the first few months she would only throw it in my face, but eventually she got it together and started feeling the kid. Lunches turned into dinner and the rest is history.

I got up to start getting dressed and I could tell that Ashlyn was boring a hole in my back. I ignored her ass because she was not about to whine me out of going out. I moved around the room and all she did was look before she finally opened her big ass mouth.

"Where are you going Roscoe? Its 10:00 pm at night. What do you have to do that requires you to leave you pregnant girlfriend at home and go out?"

"Not tonight Ashlyn, I have to go out and handle some business and I will be right back."

"What kind of business? NHG business? I don't know why you won't let that little childish gang go. You're about to have a daughter who doesn't need her father to be slain out in the streets somewhere." By now she was all up on me following me from room to room.

"Ash, chill with all of that you talking because I'm going out regardless."

"Okay, fine. When I drop, I will be going out as well. Watch me and you better not ask me any questions."

Ashlyn thought that she was getting under my skin with her idle threats, but she would be the one looking stupid in the end if she ever tried to get some get back. I didn't bother answering her, so she switched her tone.

"Baby can you just stay home tonight? It's hot outside and people are just looking for a reason to act stupid. Handle what you have to handle tomorrow and stay in with me, please?" she begged. I appeased her mood and we laid down together and watched movies, but the second she drifted off to sleep I was out the door. I put my hoodie over my head and kissed my two babies goodnight, not knowing that it would be last time saying it.

LA

SIX YEARS LATER

I sat in my home office getting topped off by a chick who was literally swallowing my shit. Her skills had me moaning and shit like a bitch, but this was nothing new for Peaches. Whenever I was stressed out or just in the mood for some A1 head, Peaches was my girl. I palmed her head as I exploded inside of her mouth. Peaches made sure not to waste a drop and she circled my tip with her tongue not leaving any of my kids to waste. She disappeared from my office for a moment and then returned with a warm rag and cleaned me up. I expected her to leave after but instead, she plopped her ass down in the chair across from me.

"What's up Peach? You got some shit on your tongue or something?" I asked.

"Well actually I do. When are you and I going to take our relationship to the next level? I mean we been fucking around for years and I think I'm ready for more."

Silence

"Well, I'm glad you got that off your mind, but you already know the answer to that. I don't do relationships period! Now you may exit." I waved her off as she looked like she wanted to say more. Peaches always tried this shit about every six months like I would change my mind or some shit. Peach was one of the bitches in my rotation that I had been

CUFFED BY A GANGSTA: LA & MOCHA

fucking with for about three years and she knew to play her role, or she would be dismissed with the quickness. I don't think she realized just how fortunate she was and here she was tripping.

I explained to her over and over that I would never be monogamous with just one female, so it was her choice to leave or stay. My veins had pumped ice ever since the day that my brother died. Me and his wifey Ashlyn begged him to not retaliate against NBK, but his pride wouldn't let him listen to us. My brother was set up by a bitch who he though was on his side, whole time she was setting him up. My brother and two of his friends died that night. Them niggas hit my brother with thirty-four shots. He couldn't even have an open casket at his funeral.

The day he died, I was put in his position and I vowed to avenge his death taking down the members of NBK one by one. The first person I started with was the grimy bitch that had set my brother up. She died a nice a slow death begging and pleading the entire time, but her cries were heard upon deaf ears. Women and children were usually untouched in my book, but that bitch was the only exception. As a shorty coming up, I despised NHG, promising to never get caught up in the gang life, but instead playing pro football. That shit is the exact opposite of my life today, I am a twenty-four-year-old man who leads the NHG. NHG had changed from back in the day. We had multiplied and ran the entire south side. We had our hands in almost everything from slinging crack, bodying niggas, stealing cars, rapping, and more. NHG rang bells in the streets and NBK was almost extinct besides a couple here and there.

I finished up some work and then made my way to NHG's monthly meeting. There was about fifty of us that met up once a month to discuss what was moving and shaking in the streets. We discussed the numbers that the chop shop was making, drug sales, and anything that was profitable for us. Each person was divided up in the operations. Everyone was getting money so there was no need for any malice or jealousy in our hearts. The reins came to me when Sco died and though I didn't want to take them, I had too. Ever since then streets had been mine.

I walked into the room and all chatter ceased upon my arrival. Niggas respected me and I wouldn't have it any other way. "Alright let's get to business. Let me hear the numbers for this month," I spoke.

Zoe, my right hand began to read out numbers for the body shop and they were unusually low. "Yo, what's going on with the shop? Ain't no cars coming in?" No one spoke up so I directed my question to the chief of the shop. "What is up Ro?" I asked.

"Yo, man, I don't know what happened this month, but word is there is a shop on the west that is charging dumb cheap. Some nigga named Meezy."

"Yo, why is this just being brought to my attention? Anything moving in this city, I should know about." I hated coming off like a tyrant to the gang, but some shit was a no brainer when it came to money and how we would be eating. I talked with the guys for another thirty minutes before we got to the news that we all had been waiting to discuss. Every year we would throw a big ass bash on Sco's birthday. That shit bought the city out. We would throw a cookout at the basketball court that we used to always hoop at, followed by a party at club Penthouse.

I ended the meeting and my boy Zoe and decided to go grab cheese steak from Ishkabibbles. Ish's was law and the chicken philly always put me in a good mood.

"Yo gang, Sco's bday bash gone be lit as usual. I hope Peaches bring her fine ass friend Lexi. That bitch got an ass like Nicki and a face like Keri, I got to have her."

"Man, you been pining over that girl for forever and still ain't got no play, I say you move on my boy," I said to Zoe.

"Nigga fuck you, just because you got hoes in rotation. I'm trying to find me a wife, ain't nobody on that bachelor shit like you gang."

"Yeah, and no one is on that lovey dovey shit. I fuck, get my dick sucked, and keep it moving," I shrugged. This caused Zoe's forehead to crease.

"You one miserable nigga," he retorted and we both laughed at the truth. We pulled up to Ish's and Raheem already knew what I wanted. The spot was pretty packed as usual, and I didn't need niggas pressing me for a job or females trying to get on, so I ordered my shit to go.

I chopped it up with Zoe and Raheem for a minute when this girl with a donkey walked in. Ass was my weakness. Her face wasn't all that cute, but that *ass* though. I imagined bending her fat ass over and dicking her out, but I wouldn't even go there. Bitches got too attached when all I wanted to do was fuck.

"Um excuse me? Are you going to stand there drooling over her, holding the line up?" An irritated woman behind me asked. I turned to face her, and she had one manicured hand on her hip waiting for me to move.

"My bad sweetheart, you can go before me," I said.

She smirked, "Sweetheart? Ohhh ok," she said stepping in front of me.

"Uhh did I say something wrong shorty?"

All she did was continue smirking while giving me the once over. "Ohhh my name is Sweetheart now, but I'm pretty sure you called me chubby before and then continued to berate me like I was nothing more than the gunk on your shoe," she said, angrily.

"Aye yo, I don't even know you, so why you tripping?"

"You don't know me? Haha, let me familiarize you then. *'Hey chubby, you really look like you could lay off the subs with your fat ass,'*" she said, in a mocking tone. I didn't know what shorty was talking about, but as I stared in her face, it all came back to me. She was the chubby chick in the McDonald's uniform that was rushing me to go about three or four years ago. Life had surely been good to her as her McDonald's uniform was replace by light blue scrubs and a doctor's coat. He acne had subsided and now her olive colored skin brightened up any room. Baby girl had been working out too, because that weight had now disappeared into muscle. She honestly reminded me of the singer Justine Sky.

Before I could get another word out, she quickly payed for her food and waltzed out of the place just like she did the first time we met.

ASHLYN

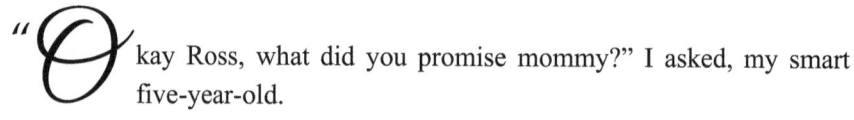

"Okay Ross, what did you promise mommy?" I asked, my smart five-year-old.

"Don't tell Uncle La that you have a boyfriend."

"And what else?"

"Don't tell him that we are moving to a new house. Mommy I promise I remember and won't tell. Can I have my juice now?" Ross asked, as she stared up at me with those big brown eyes. She was the exact replica of her dad and every time I looked at her, I saw him. I was angry and sad at the same time. I begged Sco to stay in the house that night, but he didn't listen. I cried for so long over this man, I could not get him out of my mind no matter how hard I tried. Yeah, he messed around in the streets and thought I didn't I know about it, but I loved him with every fiber of my being. I cried after my pregnancy, not even wanting to hold or touch my baby for the first couple months of her life. I went through depression as well as postpartum. My sadness then turned into anger and I cursed his name daily, blaming him for putting himself in that position to leave me and his daughter behind.

LA came and demanded that I see a therapist. At first, I never minded his idle threats until he threatened to take my baby. LA would do any and everything for his niece and he was not going to sit around and just let me neglect her. We both would stay in the dark gloomy house crying for hours; Ross because she was unfed, unclothed, and unloved; and I was just broken. LA got wind of that shit and took Ross from me until I could get my shit together. After time, healing, therapy, and prayer, I finally forgave Roscoe and started to move on with my life.

I made my way upstairs to finish getting ready. Ross had an appointment with her pediatrician and my dad aka LA would be coming to pick us up any minute now. I was older than LA but somehow, he still treated me like I was the little sister. LA stepped up in his brother's absence not missing an appointment, holiday, school play, tummy ache or anything. I threw on a striped blue and white romper, Ugg slippers and a dash of Dior perfume and was ready.

"Mommy," Ross called out. "Someone is at the door; do you want me to open it?" she asked politely.

"Ross I will let you make that decision for yourself." Ross knew daggon' well she should not be opening any door. So, I would lay back and see what she would do. I skipped down the stairs and just like I expected, Ross stood by the door, but it was unopened. "Good girl Bug," I said swooping her up into my arms and opening the door for LA.

"Uncle Laaa," Ross jumped out of my arms and hugged her uncle. Since she was little, she had been calling him La instead of LA and he let her.

"What's up, my favorite niecy poo?" he said, while tickling her. All she could do was laugh as I smiled on.

"Yoooo, sis. I hope you cooked cause a nigga starving," LA said, with a smile.

"LA when are you going to settle down and find someone who can cook you a home cooked meal?" I asked, while making him a plate of eggs, bacon, and fruit that Ross had begged me to make even though she only ate about two bites of it.

"Come on sis, you know I am not into no relationships, I don't need to bi- I mean female on me like that."

"Well you need to rethink that. Ross and I will not always be here to cook and wash your dirty drawers."

"Uncle La, where's potato? Ross asked out of the blue.

"Who Bug?" LA asked just as confused as I was.

"The lady with the-" Ross then began to stuff her shirt with pillows. LA only laughed while I was still confused.

"Aye she crazy man! She is talking about the jank Peaches," he laughed.

"LA don't be having my baby around your little groupies. You either find one woman to settle down with and make her an aunt or that's it."

"Yeah, yeah, man," he brushed me off. "Now let's go before ya'll late for her appointment. It's still on Nickerson, right?"

"No, we switched doctors, so I'll give you the address for the new place."

We piled in LA's Tesla and made it to the new location in no time. I filled out all of Ross' new patient information and sat until we were called. Ross played with some children in the playing area while I answered some work emails.

"Ross Anderson," the nurse called out. I grabbed Ross and we walked back followed by LA.

"Hi ladies, I'm nurse Hart and I'll just be taking little miss Ross' weight, height, and blood pressure."

"Okay," Ross, smiled sweetly and stepped on the scale.

"LA put your phone away," I said. He had been on his damn phone since we arrived.

"Aite man," he said, while shoving his phone in his pocket like he was irritated.

"Uncle, say hi to Ms. Hart," Ross instructed. Nurse Hart looked up from her clipboard and her smile turned into a frown as LA reached out for her hand. "You again," she said, and I was confused.

LA only smiled, and Ross and I looked on. The nurse then led to us to an exam room.

"Mommy, I have to pee," Ross said, while doing the potty dance.

"Ross, are you sure? The doctor should be in at any moment."

"Yes, mommy I'm sure! Come on let's go now!" I walked out of the room leaving the nurse and LA alone.

LA

I sat there watching the nurse avoid eye contact with me. She did anything but look at me while she scribbled on her clipboard. I clearly had shorty shook.

"Yo, you gone pretend to scribble on your paper for the whole time I'm here?" I asked.

"Yep, that's exactly what I'm going to do."

"Well if this means anything to you, I'm sorry for the way I talked to you in the past."

Silence

"Your apology is not needed," she said, plainly, never looking up.

"Well you're clearly still hurt, so I'll leave you alone."

"No one is hurt. I just do not have time for an arrogant ass like you."

"Okay, I will take that. Lay it all out for me right now. If that's what it will take for you to go out with me." I don't know why I was asking her out, but I felt really bad for the way I had treated her before, she didn't deserve that.

I had been low key thinking about shorty since the last time I had seen her at Ish's. She was so damn fine and had a head on her shoulders. I could keep her around for some time. Nurse Hart only gawked at me like she had never been asked out before.

"Soo, you gone let me take you out or no?"

"You, you," she stuttered. "You want to take me out?"

"That's what I just asked you." By now she was fidgeting, and she kept pushing her glasses up to the bridge of her nose. "You don't have to do all of that shorty, its real, this moment is real. Those feeling that you are feeling are real."

"Laaaaa, we're back," Ross came running in and jumped into my lap. That got nurse Hart off of the hook as she scurried out of the room.

"What did you do to that girl Lance?" Ash asked as if she knew that I was the reason she ran out.

"I didn't do shit to her scary ass but try to take her out and she went running."

"Well maybe you need to try a softer approach with her. She doesn't seem to be the rugged type that you are used to. Be a gentleman and most of all be nice," Ash preached.

I guess she was right, I had to play it a little different with her timid ass and that is just what I was going to do.

MOCHA

I finally made it home after doing a thirty-six-hour shift. Working at a hospital was no joke, but every day that I was able to help save someone made it all worth it. And who would've thought that the boy that had made me cry and ran me out of the joint four years ago would pop back in my life like a damn boomerang at my damn job? And don't get me started on how I acted when I finally came face to face with his ass, I totally lost it. I waited for the day when I would be able to show him that I wasn't the sad frumpy girl that he remembered, but it didn't go that way. I don't know if it was his dreamy brown eyes, his copper colored skin, or his gorgeous locks that were always neatly twisted every time I ran into him, but he kind of did something to me.

    I removed my scrubs and tossed them into the laundry basket and headed to the shower. I knew a scalding hot shower would put me right to sleep. I stripped naked and searched my body in the wall sized mirror for a blemish or scar, but none appeared. No pimple no stretch mark or anything. I had worked hard for this body, working out twice a day for the last five years to achieve a body that only Instagram models had. Though, I looked good on the outside, my self-esteem had always been low, and I couldn't see my beauty. Everyone always gave me compliments and I'd had boyfriends in the past, but my confidence is why my relationships never lasted.

First there was Mikey, he treated me like a queen, but he was bomb himself, light skin with pretty eyes. That shit got the best of me and I became jealous and possessive which led to the ending of that. Then there was my most recent relationship with Kenny, and this nigga played on my self-esteem and cheated on me with every girl in the book. He would call me names and tell me that no other man would have me. I'm originally from Virginia, so I left there and decided to apply to a hospital in Philly all in an attempt to get away from Kenny and his berating ways. I had spent summer's here anyway with my family, so it was only right, I left Kenny and made Philly my home.

I stepped into the steaming water and it relaxed me. I knew that afterwards I would fall asleep like a little baby. I stayed in for about thirty minutes until I resembled a raisin. I lotioned down with my favorite Native Banana Cream Lotion and slid right in the bed, ass naked. The moment I felt myself drifting off, my phone rang, and it was my crazy ass cousin Pisces. Pisces and I were close as hell and I even spent summers in Philly with her and her family. P and I were total opposites, but I guess that is what made us click.

"Hello," I said groggily.

"Yo', what's up bitch? I know you not sleep," she boomed into the phone.

"Yes, P, I am sleep, so how can I help you?"

"Girl you such an old lady, either you are working or home sewing some shit," P always joked about my crochet habit, but I could care less. "Again, P what do you want? I know you didn't call just to insult me."

"You right, I really called to see if you would come out with me tomorrow night. Before you say no, yo' ass can sleep the whole day and then come out with me tomorrow. You know you need to find a man and I'm definitely about to get with one of them NHG niggas."

"NHG? What is that a gang or something?" I hadn't been to Philly since I started college, so I was lost.

"You damn right. The most popping gang in Philly. All them niggas ballers."

"Girl, how are you looking for someone else when you already have a man and a gang banger at that?" I asked, bewildered.

"Girl, Rod, is so last week. Pinky P is single and ready to mingle,'" she joked. That was Just like Pisces to run a guy dry and then when all of the loot was gone, she would bounce.

"Well girl, I'm going to sleep now toodles," I said.

"Noooooo, bitch, you didn't say whether you going with me or not."

Silence

"I guess, I'll go, but drinks on you."

"Girl, hell to the no. Drinks going to be on them gump ass niggas."

I couldn't help but laugh at the mess that this girl was about to get me into.

ASHLYN

I did a once over in the mirror at the skin tight black latex dress that I was wearing. I wanted to give a *eat your heart out* look, but not an *I'm fucking tonight* look. I was meeting up with my secret boo while Ross was staying with her nana tonight and LA would be picking her up the next day. I felt like I had to keep him a secret because LA would lose it. For some reason he thought that I was supposed to stay loyal to his dead brother. It wasn't fair because, like what? *I was just supposed to live the rest of my life alone?* On top of that, I had received a job offer in Alaska that I was really considering. It was a director of sales position making $65,000 a year. My dilemma was that LA wouldn't let me leave that easily halfway across the country with his only niece, so I made sure that Ross didn't say anything to him.

I heard a knock on my door, and I glanced at myself in my mirror before getting the door. I opened the door and faced Shaud, my secret boyfriend. He smiled brightly and took me into his embrace. I loved everything about him, but I couldn't find the gall to introduce him to everyone.

"Hey beautiful," he said while handing me a bouquet of roses.

"Hey, Shaud. Thank you so much for the flowers. Would you like a glass of wine before we go?"

"Yes, that would be nice."

"Red or white?" I asked.

"Red," he answered while surveying the art on my walls. Shaud had never been in my home for as long as we had been creeping, which was three months to be exact. I poured him and I a glass and then cozied up to him on the couch. We had about an hour before our dinner reservations.

"You are beautiful," Shaud, said while pecking my cheek. Shaud was what one would call pretty and dapper. He had a sandy hue, with curly hair and the most impeccable golden eyes. He was the opposite of Roscoe as he worked as a litigator at a brokerage firm. For the last three months he had showed me that he was all about me from the moment that I spilled my coffee on him at this quaint little breakfast spot. He smiled while I incessantly apologized and by the end of the day, he was calling me asking me out for breakfast the next day. That was our thing. Every day at 7:15 am we would meet for coffee at the same spot before work.

"You're not so bad yourself," I said, giving him a smile.

"Where is little mama?" he asked, referring to Ross.

"She is out with my mother."

"Well I cannot wait to meet her," he said, while finishing off his wine. That made me a little uneasy because Ross was a straight up snitch. She wasn't even supposed to know about Shaud, but she caught me face timing him one night when her little butt was supposed to have been sleeping. I just didn't know when I would show Shaud to the world, but he was starting to question me more and more about it and I couldn't continue to hide it for long.

"I'm sure you will meet her soon, but let's get out of here," I said, trying to change the conversation.

"Okay, I know you don't want me to meet your daughter yet, but eventually I will, right? Her and the rest of your family. I'm not into being someone's little secret Ashlyn," he said defensively.

"I know, I know, and you're not a secret to me. There are just some things I need to work out, okay?" I said, sincerely. Shaud kissed my lips and nodded his head in understanding. Now I just had to get some gall to tell LA because I didn't want to lose out on Shaud. The famous line from "Waiting to Exhale" kept playing in my head. *That is a good man Savannah.*

MOCHA

*P*isces had come to my house early in the morning so that we could go and get pampered before our night out. I didn't understand why she was so pressed, but she said that it was a must that we get our, hair, nails, toes and eyebrows done. After getting all of that and spending about $250, we still had to go shopping and that took even longer. Everything that I picked out, Pisces said that it was not sexy enough and that I needed to show some of my chocolate skin. I wasn't the girl who dressed very provocatively, so at the end I decided on a brown and black Fendi button up, a black vinyl skirt and black patent black ankles boots. I accented my face with a bold wine-colored lipstick, and Fenty foundation with Anastasia highlighter and blush. All these things came from my closet, so I didn't spend a dime in the mall.

I walked out of the house to see that Pisces had on a fuck me dress that had holes all through the dress which made her ass practically hang out. Her makeup was a little too dramatic and her 40-inch bundles bounced with a wavy curl.

"What's up bitch? You ready to go snag a baller tonight?" Pisces greeted me.

I didn't really want to snag anyone, but I obliged just to make her happy. We pulled up to the club and as I expected it was nice and packed, making us have to park way in ump dump land. By the time we reached the Front of the club my dogs were barking, and I was glad that I wore my hair in a bun because it would sweat out by now. I tried not to look like the girls whose feet met the door before they did. Now, I Needed a drink even though drinking was a rarity for me. We made it into the club after paying $25. Pisces claimed she knew so many people and we would get in for free but that never happened.

"Girl look at all of the ballers in this bitch. Ohhhh oh and look over there! NHG is in the building, I definitely have to find my way into their section," she was going on and on like a damn fan.

"P, chill out, let's just have fun tonight. Men are not that scarce for you to be acting like this."

"Girl please. You need a man, so we gone find your grumpy ass some dick tonight." P then walked off to the bar with me following behind her. Once we got there, this cute dude with a Bulls jersey approached Pisces and offered to buy her a drink. Instead of accepting and thanking him, she gave him the stank face, took the drink and walked off. I apologized to him with my eyes and grabbed my cucumber martini. I found myself looking down at myself just to make sure I looked okay. I felt like I had a little muffin top, so I practically sucked my Stomach in until I was uncomfortable. I was not the hugest thing at a size six, but I also wasn't the smallest.

Just as I checked myself in my compact mirror, I locked eyes with the infamous LA on the second floor in a section. His stare enticed me that I couldn't look away. He them motioned for me to come up and I was losing it, like why would he want me to come up there with him. I was not the Instagram beauty type of girl that he was probably use to.

"Girl, did you just see LA tell me to come up to his section? Come on girl lets go. This is his brother birthday party." I let Pisces believe that he was waving at her and followed her up to the section. To say that it was packed was an understatement. There had to be about fifty men there all dripped out in ice wearing R.I.P Sco shirts.

"What's up lil' mama? You want a drink?" Some beefy dude asked, the name Nuke was inscribed on his silver fronts. I had just finished my martini, so I was ready for another. I smiled politely and said yes, and he came back with a glass of Ace of Spades. "Thank you," I said.

"No problem, where you from I haven't ever see you in here and I'm part owner of the club."

"Ohh, I don't come out much and I'm originally from Virginia."

"Okay, okay two up two down," he laughed. I turned around to see where Pisces had gone, and she was in the middle of three guys laughing her ass off. I made sure to keep an eye on her wild self.

"So, this is your spot," I continued the conversation with a dude who I learned to be Nuke.

"Yep this all me an-" he started, but then smiled at me and walked away. That was rude as hell and I didn't know what I had said to make him just walk away from me in the middle of a conversation. Now, I was all alone so I decided to hop on social media so I wouldn't look too bored. About five minutes later another dude bumped into me and almost knocked me over.

"Oh, my bad baby." The dude said while helping his drunk friend D off of the ground. "My mans a lil' lit tonight, I didn't mean to almost knock you over." He smiled and showed them pearly whites and I was in love. He looked good all around.

"Oh, it's okay," I replied while smiling. I was about to say something else when he just abruptly walked off. Something was up with me tonight, I mean, did my breath stink or something because I had never scared two men off in one night. Now I was ready to go so I texted P.

This girl had a nerve to look at the text and left me on read, so I decided to go downstairs without her ass. "Hold up, hold where you are going?" I heard a familiar voice, say while grabbing my arm.

"Don't grab me," I said while snatching away from LA.

"Damn baby, calm down no one Is trying to hurt you, I was just wondering why you are running off."

"I am not running off; I just don't want to be up here anymore."

"Oh, so you mad cause I was running them nigga's away?"

"Huh?" I asked, unsure of what he was talking about.

"He smirked and stroked his beard and I noticed how good he looked tonight. His dreads were twisted dreads lay wildly in his face, and he wore a gold and red bulls jersey over a fitted hoodie, black Balmain jeans and off-white sneakers.

"Them two niggas that just approached you, I told them you were off limits," he continued.

"And why in the world would you do that?" I quizzed.

"Because, I want you," he flashed those platinum fronts off and continued stroking his beard. I didn't know what to say. He was so bold and caught me totally off guard.

"Oooh okay," I managed to get out.

"Okay, you gone go out with me or will I have to keep running niggas off until I get to you?"

I smiled causing my one dimple on my right cheek to show. That shit only happened when I was smiling hard as hell.

"What's up LA? I been looking for your fine ass all night," I heard my loud ass cousin approaching.

"Wassup," he said, and then turned his attention back to me. "What's your math baby?" he asked. I was so confused as I looked at him blankly.

"Math?"

"Your phone number baby, your phone number," I felt a little slow as I rattled it off to him.

"Ummmm, Mocha, I'm ready to go!" Pisces said, with a sudden attitude out of nowhere.

"Really, Pisces we've only been here for an hour."

"Girl niggas is wack and broke and I'm ready to go," she said, marching past me.

I smiled at LA, before chasing after her. I didn't get why she was all of a sudden so irritated. Once we got to the car, she went on and on about how NHG were so broke and just a bunch of bangers. But it was so crazy to me because for the past few days she had been praising them. Someone out of the crew must have rejected her. I just stayed quiet until she dropped me off. I showered but as I tried to go to sleep, it just wouldn't come to me.

I decided to text LA since he had texted me letting me know his number. It was about 2:30 am, so I'm guessing the club would have just let out.

"Hey, its Mocha, be safe out there and have a goodnight," I texted.

I didn't know what was going on or why I was being so bold, but I was just going to go with it because usually I was so uptight. Less than ten minutes later, I received a text back from him.

"Yo, what is up?" I thought you was gone block my number or some shit but I'm glad you didn't lol. I just dropped my boys off now, I'm about to take my black ass home. You vamping with me tonight?"

"Vamping?"

"Yeah, like staying up."

"Ohhh, yeah, I guess until I can fall asleep. Usually I am at work right now, so my brain won't let me sleep."

"Oh word, I guess you was just filling in the other day when you saw my niece, huh?

"Correct, I go to different departments, but my specialty is Pediatrics"

After that text, LA didn't text back for about thirty minutes before he FaceTimed me. He claimed he like to talk versus texting and for the rest of the night we talked until the sun came up. It was literally 6:00 am before I went to sleep, and I was out. LA and I learned a lot about each other that night and though he was in a gang I chose not to judge him. After we hung up, I couldn't wait to call Pisces, but I knew she would still be sleep. I had to tell her that LA and I would be meeting up the next day for lunch. I knew my cousin would be so happy that I had finally taken interest in a man. I just couldn't wait to fill her in.

LA

I walked into my OG's house and was met with the smell of turkey wings, greens, macaroni and cheese, yams and buttered rolls. Mama was still cooking Sunday dinner every Sunday for just me and her. My Pop's had died a year ago and my brothers were gone, so it was just us eating on left overs for days.

I snuck up on her as she hummed some old gospel song. She was stirring her greens as I pecked her cheeks. "Lance Anderson, if, you don't take off that cap in my house," she barked.

"Ma, my dreads need to be re-twisted. You gone do them for me?"

"Uhh uhh, nope. You better get one of them fast girls you been running around with to do it."

"Man, them hoes want to do more than my hair, so I will pass," I laughed.

"Well don't be calling them hoes now because you used to love them. I can't count how many girls came knocking at my door saying they were pregnant with your baby. I wish you would just settle down son, you not getting any younger," she turned to me as I smiled a little. My mam acted like I was thirty or something.

"Who is she son? I haven't seen that smile since your first and last girlfriend Jania."

"Ain't nobody ma, gone head."

"Boy, you are not fooling me, somebody got your nose wide open."

I listened to my mom as I thought of Mocha, I wouldn't say my nose was open, but I was feeling her. She was so smart and soft spoken, but that is what drew me to her. I was used to live wire girls who never shut the fuck up. I didn't know where Mocha and I would go since we had Only been talking for two days, but I could see something with her. She wasn't bad on the eyes either, soft chocolate skin, deep brown eyes, and a bottom half that looked like it belonged to a horse. She was all around beautiful even though I could tell that she was a little insecure.

"Ma, I did meet a girl. A really good girl. She a nurse and shit."

"Well if she is a good girl, don't go tainting her."

"Ma, I could never taint her. She too strong for that. We talked on the phone for hours and she not gone let me play her even if I wanted to." Just talking about her made me text her.

"Mo, what's good I know we supposed to be linking up but, My OG in here throwing down in the kitchen and we def can't eat all of it. You want a plate?"

"Ohhh Mo? You giving me nicknames already lol but I'm at work and will not be off until tomorrow morning, (Sad face emoji)

"Well what time is your break? I can bring it to you if that is okay."

"Okay, cool. My break is at eleven pm. See you then!"

About three hours later, I was on my way to the hospital to meet Mocha. She told me to meet her in the cafeteria and when I got there she was laughing with some Doctor. I didn't want to interrupt so I just observed them. She leaned in laughing with him while he periodically stroked her back. He then whispered something into her ear that really made her chuckle. I know I shouldn't have been getting so flustered, but I wanted to know what the fuck was so funny too.

When she finally spotted me, she smiled and waved before strolling over in her animal covered scrubs. "Hey, there," she greeted cheerfully."

"Yo," I said, standing to pull her chair out.

"The food smells so good, I can't wait to dig in to it."

I guess she noticed my silence.

"You okay, you're kind of quiet tonight," she said.

"I'm good, just tired."

"Ohh ok," she said, while forking the macaroni and cheese. "Oh my god, this is sooo good. Mama gone have to give me some lessons." My OG spot wasn't far from the hospital do it was still warm.

I slightly chucked, but I couldn't get her and that damn wack ass doctor off of my mind." I saw you over there with the yellow dude, ya'll friends?"

"Oh my god Lance, is that why you're over here looking like you want to kill someone. Dr. Sumner is just a mentor. He is married and have about six kids. I'm so good on him."

"He might not feel the same way though, that's what I be trying to tell females. Niggas be on some other shit."

"Well you don't have to worry about that and besides, I have my eye on someone else anyway."

"Yeah, me too," I smiled, while getting lost into her aura. She even had a little piece of Yam o her lip, but she was still beautiful. I took my chance and kissed her and surprisingly, she kissed me back. At that moment I knew that she was going to be my girl.

PISCES

*J*almost threw up in my mouth as my cousin went on and on about the nigga that was supposed to be my man. Mocha had the nerve to get with LA when I told her that I wanted him and now she had the nerve to tell me that he had been bringing her lunch and shi.t I could've rung her neck through the phone if I wasn't lying next to his right hand Zoe. I called myself trying to get close to LA ass and ended up with his homeboy's dick in my ass. Now I had to find another way to LA without my cousin blocking me.

"Girl, you sound like you love that nigga already," I laughed.

"No, it's definitely not love, but it is a strong like. We been kicking it for two weeks straight."

"Well, I thought you said you didn't like gang bangers and he definitely bang."

"I mean that's a part of his life that he does not want me in in because it's too dangerous, so I just go with the flow. There are certain things about me that I keep private too."

"What? That you had an eating disorder and still make yourself throw up to this day." I didn't mean to sound so harsh, but she needed to get that LA was not the type of guy that she needed.

Silence

"Yo, get your ass off of the phone with that gossiping shit!" Zoe yelled. "Go wash yo' ass or something, you been laying with my cum over you all night."

"Boy, go to hell," I said, back "Girl I will call you later," I said to Mocha and hung up the phone abruptly.

"Nigga, you always talking shit when I get on the phone."

"Cause that's all you do, and you wonder why you will never be my girl!" he yelled.

"Nigga please, I said, as he walked away a little bitch. Little did he know, if things didn't work out with LA and I, I would be using the turkey baster on that ass.

LA

I waited in the parking lot for Zoe late ass, I swear he was just like a bitch making me wait for him every time we had to be somewhere. Some new shipment had come to the warehouse and we needed to make sure everything was there. I didn't trust anyone but Zoe fucking around with thousands of dollars' worth of stolen shit that needed to be sold.

While I waited for his snail ass, I smiled at Mocha's incessant good girl act. I know it would be a while before we fucked so I asked her to send me a pic of that ass, I don't know why girls hated sending nudes. I wish that I could see her face right now because I know she was flustered. The velvety skin was probably glowing like hell. I knew she wouldn't send one, but I had to fuck with her.

"Lance find you something to do," she replied.

"I want to do you," I texted back

Bye was her last text before Zoe finally came running.

"Yo, bro look at this shit here," he said, finally getting to me. He handed me his phone and it appeared that some niggas were on Facebook live. It was about five people yelling fuck NHG and at first I didn't care what the fuck they were saying until I heard one lil' nigga say, "Yeah ya'll we over here smoking on that dead OOP Roscoe."

My fucking head was on fire as them niggas repeatedly spoke on my dead brother. There weren't too many things that got me upset, but mentioning Sco and CJ was a fucking no, no. I was ready to ride out and Zoe read my mind.

We rode until we reached the west side, looking for them NBK niggas. The thing about the west side was that their projects were gated so there was no way for us to get in without someone noticing. Not that we were scared, but two niggas against twenty wouldn't work. We rode past the corner store and on the other side I noticed one of the guys that was in the live video was posted up. In the video he wasn't saying much, but in my mind, he was guilty by association. I grabbed the rugger from my lap and aimed it at his head. Just as I was about to pull the trigger, my phone chimed. It was Mocha, I was about to ignore that shit so I could handle this fool, but I was instantly stopped when I glance back and saw two undercover cops sitting at the corner. What was the point of them being undercover if a hood nigga like me noticed them?

"Shit," Zoe and I cursed simultaneously. Being careful about not looking suspicious, we quietly left the scene, but it wasn't over by a long shot. Shit was gone get handled. As I rode to take Zoe back home Mocha popped in my head again, for real, if she wouldn't have texted my phone, I would have never looked back and saw the boys behind us. I guess in a way she saved my ass from doing twenty to life.

"Hellllloo big head," she sang, after I hit her up.

"My bad, I couldn't answer your call earlier, I was kinda tied up."

"Umm, tied up. Not doing anything crazy right?"

I lied to appease her, "Naw, not for real. Just handling business"

Silence

"What's up Mo, why you so quiet?" I asked.

"I really don't know, and I know that this is none of my business, but I know that you bang. I'm all too familiar with the gang life and how people lose their life because of it. I guess what I'm trying to say is that I want you to be safe and before you think of doing something stupid, remember your mom and your little niece who need you. And think about me too," she said softly.

Damn, I wanted to keep that part of my life private from Mo, but eventually she would find out anyway. I mean we were the most The Notorious

Hiita' Gang for Christ sake. "Mo, I can't make any promises to you, but I will be as careful as I can be and don't worry about be shorty, I made it this far." I knew that I could not sugar talk Mocha because she was a smart girl, she knew when I was bullshittin' her, so I chose to be upfront with her.

Silence

"So, you ready to let me come see your crib or what? You don't have any excuses today do you?"

"Nope, actually I don't so come through, but leave your horny thoughts at home," she giggled through the phone.

"Yo ass must is gone to wearing a paper bag or something."

"LA, shut up and just come on before I change my mind."

"Aye yo, don't call me LA. My government name is reserved for you and my mama," I said seriously. She didn't even sound right saying it sounding all proper and shit. LA was my street name and she was a little more special than that.

MOCHA

I paced around trying to make sure that my place was spotless before LA came over. I had a lavishly decorated town house in Narberth which was about thirty minutes outside of South Philly but, I hadn't really cleaned up in a few weeks due to my strenuous work schedule. I tidied up as much as I could and lit a few Cashmere woods candles to give the place a nice scent. I couldn't wear a paper bag to keep LA off me, so I chose Abercrombie and fitch sweats and a matching shirt. The pants still hugged my curves, but LA would just have to keep his hand to himself.

Twenty minutes Later, LA was standing at my door with a Netflix and chill kind of vibe; he had even brought snacks and take out Thai food.

"Yo spot almost nicer than mine," he commented.

"Almost? Yeah, I bet," I laughed.

"You got Netflix?" he asked.

"Yea who doesn't have Netflix? the only thing I don't have is chill," I busted out laughing before I could even finish the joke while he just stood there smirking. "Okay, okay that joke was lame, so what," I continued laughing. My phone then started to ring and it was Pisces. I thought of just not answering, but something could've been wrong, so I excused myself and went to my room.

"What P?" I answered, still a little tight about her smart comments before.

"Girl, what are you doing and why are you whispering?"

"I'm minding my business and I am talking low because LA is here, and I don't want him to hear me just in case I have to cuss your ass out."

"Damn every time I talk to you LA is in the picture. Let me find out you the type to dip on your friends and family when you finally get a man."

I looked at the phone because this girl was absolutely going crazy. That's exactly the type of girl that she was, not me.

"Look, P I have company, so I have to go."

"Okay girl well call me later. I really have something important to tell you."

"Okay." *Click.* I could not wait to hang up with her. She had been so negative lately and I didn't have time for it. I turned around to go back to LA and he was creeping up right behind me which scared the crap out of me.

"Oh my god LA. I mean Lance. You scared the crap out of me."

"Why you up here whispering? He asked calmly and I noticed he had just got a nice edge up and his dreads were in a top knot. The fragrance he wore enticed me and his simple look was pleasing to my eyes. He wore blue Balmain jeans, a white V-neck with wheat timberland boots.

"Um, I was not whispering. I was talking to my cousin Pisces." LA was now invading my space as his warm breath tickled my nose.

"Why you are stuttering?" he asked softly. By now he had me just where he wanted me, under his trance. A thin layer of sweat formed along my brow and LA only smiled.

"Lay down," he in structed meme. My mind was telling me no, but my body wouldn't listen. I laid down on my back, awaiting what was next. "Take off your pants and your panties."

I slowly got up and peeled my pants and boy shorts down, never breaking eye contact with him. My freshly waxed peach was exposed as I tried covering it.

"Don't do that!" LA barked and it turned me on. "Lay down and play with that pussy for me."

Now I was caught off guard, "Huh?" I head myself saying.

"You heard me, now lay down and make that pussy cream for me."

I laid down and he instructed me to insert one finger into me and then two. "Go in and out slowly," he demanded while watching me like a hawk. I felt a little stupid masturbating in front of him, but then it started to feel good as I inserted a third finger and went around and around in a circular motion. I locked eyes back with LA while I hungrily liked my lips thinking that he would join me. He never moved from his spot as I started to pump my hips onto my fingers, imagining it was him inside of me.

"Aahhh shit," I moaned as the creamy fluid dripped from me. Breathless and horny as hell, I got up and walked to LA, but he stopped me mid-stride.

"Now put your clothes on so we can go and Netflix since you don't have no chill in you. I just taught you how to please yourself until you really ready for this dick." With that he walked away leaving me standing there. I couldn't believe his ass, never had I ever masturbated, especially not in front of someone and now he had me looking stupid and naked. He would give in soon enough and when he was ready, I would be ready.

I woke up on the couch by myself. I guess LA had slipped out when I had fell asleep. For the rest of the night we ate, cuddled and watched Movies until we both fell asleep. I got up and disposed of the empty food containers and bottles. I couldn't help but smile just thinking of LA, he hated when I called him that, but I loved it. I thought that I would be single for the rest of my life, but he came along and changed my mind.

I remember talking to my mom about the boy who had called me fat at Ish's, but who would have known what that rude boy and I would have become. I turned on Toni Braxton's epic *The Essential Toni Braxton* album and began to do some deep cleaning. I started cleaning walls and everything while singing my life out to Toni's "I Love Me Some Him". I got through the entire CD and my house was damn near spotless. I headed to the shower to wash the bleach and Pine sol off me when my phone rung, again it was Pisces.

"Hey, P?" I greeted.

"I need to talk are you busy?" she sounded a bit off.

"Nope, I'm listening."

"Well I didn't want to tell you this because I knew that you were feeling LA, but LA and I were into each other last year and we had sex."

My Brow crinkled because P had never mentioned this to me before.

"Pisces, are you serious? Stop playing around."

"I'm not playing Mocha, we were really feeling each other, we only ended it because I broke it off when I thought that I was moving out of town. That shit really fucked his head up. Why do you think he ignores me when he sees me? He hates me to this day. He said that me and Jania, his ex were the only girls that he ever loved."

"So, you mean to tell me that you two were in a full-fledged relationship and neither one of you muthafuckers thought to tell me," I was pissed. I hardly ever cursed.

"I mean, I knew you was feeling him and didn't want to hurt your feelings, but when I saw that you were falling so hard, I had to let you in," she said, sounding as if she was about to break out in tears and P never cried.

"Well I'm glad, we didn't get too far. Damn P! I wish you would've told me this shit earlier." I certainly do not want a man that my cousin used to fuck on, so whatever LA and I were doing is officially over. I thought about confronting him, but P advised me against it and to just lose contact with him, so that is exactly what I planned to do. He probably thought he was all Kinds of sweet that he was messing with two cousins, but little did he know that is ass was caught. A little part of me thought that P was just jealous, but she wouldn't lie about something like this. As shady as she was, she wasn't that low.

ASHLYN

I drove to pick up my baby from LA's house. He and I stayed practically stayed in different states, well that's how the forty-minute drive to the south suburbs. That's how private he was, only his inner circle knew where he lived, not one girl had ever been there but his one ex Jania, who abruptly left him a few years ago.

I finally made it there and I felt like I needed a nap after the drive When I walked in there was Zoe sitting front and center on the couch watching a basketball game. Zoe was kind of cute with his caramel skin and muscles that bulged out of the t-shirt he was wearing. "Hey, Zoe," where LA and my baby?

"They round back 'phew."

"Oh okay," I answered and headed to the back.

"Aye when you gone stop playing with me Ashlyn. I been chasing you since I was a kid and you just keep trying to play me."

"Zo, you must be high. You are only playing yourself," I said sassily and continued to the back only for Zoe to step in front of me.

"Who you talking to like that?" he asked, like the savage he was. "Yo cute ass scared as hell. I'm not gone stop till I get you, eventually you will get tired of running."

"Mommy, mommy," I heard. Along with the pitter patter of little feet.

Zoe made some distance between us right before Ross and LA came in. "Hey Bug," I said, while picking her up. "What were you doing out back? I missed you."

"Me and Uncle La were flying kites," her little sweet voice said.

"Uncle La and I, Bug," I said, correcting her. "Now go get your bag so we can go."

She raced upstairs and I turned my attention to LA. "My baby texted me and told me you left with some girl the other day. Who's the newest flavor of the week?"

"Ain't no flavor of the week sis," peep how he called me sis. "This one a keeper, I think he in love," Zoe chimed in.

"Whaaaat? Not the thot LA." I gasped.

"Both of ya'll need some business, yes I have a lil numba, but we just chilling. Ain't nothing for ya'll to be worried about. And what about you nigga? LA turned to Zoe. "Don't think the crew don't know about and Pisces. Nigga you not low."

Pisces! What the hell would he be doing with that girl. She practically fucked the entire NHG. He and I had some talking to do. "Oh, Pisces huh. She's classy." There was a twinge of jealousy in my voice even though I had a man. Zoe only smirked and waved me off.

"I'm ready mommy," Ross came yelling. We said our goodbyes and then we were headed home. "Mom are we going to get ice cream today? she asked for the millionth time. She knew that we went to get ice cream every Sunday, yet she still asked. "No Bug, no ice cream today," I played with her. I glanced back in the rearview mirror and she was sitting in her Booster seat, arms folded, and her little bottom lip poked out. Her face only brightened when she saw that we were reaching Baskin Robins.

When we finally got in, it was a little crowed for a Sunday as we waited in line. A little young boy took our order. Ross ordered the strawberry French toast ice-cream with sprinkles and I got basic cookies and cream. We went to sit down, and I got Ross settled and quickly went to get napkins, when I heard a familiar voice. I looked up to see a smiling Shaud' hand and hand with a woman. Just as I was about to go over and say hi, two little girls came dashing behind them and one said, "I want chocolate daddy," and he beamed at her.

Now if I'm not mistaken, Shaud had never even told me about any kids and from the shiny band that he was now sporting on his left hand told me that the fool was also married. It's not even like I went after him. This nigga begged me for months before I even let him come to my house. As I stared, he passionately kissed his wife and patted her bottom. He then whispered something in her ear. I bet the dog was saying "I'ma fuck you so good when we get home."

My heart sank and not because I was sad, but more so disappointed. Shaud was the first man that I had fully opened up to since the death of my child's father and this is how it turned out. I'm so glad that we hadn't had sex, but I wasted time and energy. No longer able to stay fixated on him I swooped Ross up and we left. She could eat her ice cream in the car. Once I got home, I chilled with Ross for a bit, bathed her and then put her to bed. Next, I called the only person that I was able to vent to over the years, who always listened no matter how early or late I called. The phone didn't even ring for ten seconds before he answered.

"What's up future baby mama?"

"Hey Zoe, can you talk?"

LA

I drifted in and out of ecstasy as Peach rode my dick like a damn cow girl all the while saying nasty shit like, "Ohhh I feel this big black dick in my stomach and, "Nut all in this fat pussy." That shit wouldn't be happening on my wife, my pull-out game was too serious. I had decided a week ago that it would be my last time fucking with Peaches, but I changed my mind since ole girl started moving funny. She hadn't been answering my calls or nothing and I was not about to chase her ass, so I let her do her. I did kind of miss her though, that ugly ass laugh where she snorted a lil' bit and the way she said LA even though I told her a million times not to call me that.

I didn't even know what I did to her ass. One week we were seeing each other every day and the next week she was ghosting me. It felt a little funny because that was usually how I did bitches and now she was doing the same to me. I had to laugh at Karma's dusty ass interfering in my shit.

I bust all over peaches mouth and then she had the nerve to lean forward and tried to kiss me. It wasn't even that she had sampled my cum, but she and I never kissed her so I didn't know why she thought the shit would change today.

"Damn LA my Pussy don't bite no more? You were in the zone the whole time we were fucking," she snapped.

"Yo I'm not trying to argue with you today, matter fact this my last time fucking you," her face dropped.

"Damn, I heard you had a new bitch, but I didn't know she had you moving like this." "Yo don't refer to her as a bitch and yea I'm moving differently, something you could never get me to do. Now look, I don't want this to end badly, but we have to stop. I got some shit going on right now and you deserve better then fucking me every once in a while, without me giving you nothing back in return. I turned to my safe and then gave her a stack of money. It had to be at least $10,000. She looked at me with disdain.

"Nigga, you out of your mind if you just think you can throw me a few dollars and I will just disappear-"

I stopped her before she could go on with her little rant. I never put my hands-on women, but this one needed to feel it. I grabbed her arm so she could hear me clearly. "That's exactly what the fuck I expect you to do. Now fuck with me if you want to. Get yo' shit and step before I hurt your lil' ass." she picked up her clothes and then left my second apartment. She was crying her ass off, but I didn't care about them damn tears. She knew we were just fucking and would never be with each other like that. Besides, I had a shorty now or did.

MOCHA

I decided to get out of the house sulking over what could've been between Lance and I and went to get a mani/pedi. I needed some color in my life, so I went for a bold yellow with little crystals lined around the edges. I even went a little longer and tried the coffin shape. This was definitely a no, no since I was a nurse, but I would cut them down after a week or so.

LA had been calling me like crazy and I would never answer. I even saw him creeping around my house at times. I just wasn't ready to let go the thought of him and I, so I avoided him and only stuck with the good memories of him. I talked to my mom about the situation and she told me that I did owe him some explanation as to why I had deaded him and she suggested that I listen to his side of the story. As far as I was concerned, he didn't have a side. He had sex with my cousin last year and that was that.

I sat bask in the chair to get my feet done and turned on the back massager when this beautiful woman walked into the shop a fuchsia pant romper with ruffles at the bottom. She was bad as hell and I was surprised when she came sat beside me and struck up a conversation. I was surprised because most people usually looked past a basic girl like me.

"Ooh girl, that color is the bomb, especially since it's about to be warm," she commented.

"Oh thanks, it's something different for me. I usually stick to nudes," I commented back.

"Girl, nude is not for a pretty bitch like you," metallics and neons seem like your style. I'm Peaches by the way. What is your name?

"Oh, I'm Mocha," I said, releasing my strawberry Frappuccino, so that I could shake her hand."

"You come to this shop all the time? This is my first time, but I heard it is butta," she said.

"Yeah I come here every other week. They get me right every time."

"Girl. why you sound so down, you look good if that helps," she went on. Her personality was so loud that it almost overpowered me.

"Well I am a little down, but I know you don't want to hear my drama."

"Girl, talk that shit out."

"Well long story short, I was really feeling this guy, but he was not who I thought he was."

"Damn girl, it be like that. I was fucking with this nigga from NHG and he been acting funny too lately."

My ears peeked up at the mention of NHG. I guess the rumors were true, the gang was just that infamous.

"Girl, I am too familiar with NHG," I said not giving her too much. I mean, I had just met her fifteen minutes ago. The Asian lady put the last of the gel top coat on my toes and I was done.

"Oh, girl if you don't mind. Let me get your number or something. You seem like a cool female and maybe we can hang out sometimes."

I looked at her for a minute and her niceness kind of scared me, but I gave her my number anyway. I needed friends other than my cousin and my work associates and Peaches seemed fun. I locked my number into her phone and then she texted me so that I would have her number.

I got home at about 3:30pm which meant that I could get a little cat nap before my overnight shift tonight at six. I was ten minutes into my nap, slobbing and all and my phone continuously buzzed back to back. Without looking. I answered. "Helloo!" I answered voice full of irritation.

"Yo, why the fuck you haven't been answering your phone?" LA yelled, almost busting ear drum.

I sat up oblivious to why I hadn't checked before I answered, but he was on the phone now so I may as well get the shit out of the way. "Calm down when you are talking to me."

"Calm down, I feel like breaking your fucking neck. What's up with you?"

"Just answer this one question for me and do not lie. You and my cousin got something going on?" I asked seriously.

"Your cousin? he repeated. "Hell naw, this why you been ignoring me over some bullshit gossip?"

"It's not gossip if I got it straight from the source you may want to think twice before lying to me."

"Man, ain't nobody got to lie to you. I don't and ain't never fucked with your cousin and that's how you gotta take it or leave it."

"I don't have to take anything. And since you seem to be so bleak about this conversation don't call me again!

"Baby, I mean, Mo, yo' cousin is lying if she told you that shit," he started to calm down so now I was open to listening.

"And?" I questioned.

"And what? What else do you want me to say? I did not fuck the bitch."

"So, you are telling me she just made up this whole story about yawl being together and ya'll breaking up because she had to move?"

"Damn right she lying, and you a dumb ass to believe any of that shit."

"You the only dumb one, just gotta stick your dick in every girl you see. I'm glad I didn't have sex with your nasty ass. Hear me clear, don't ever contact me again. Now who is the one looking stupid?" I hung up on him and then blocked each number he continued to call me back from. LA and I were officially ovaaaa'.

PEACHES

*L*A just didn't know my skills when it came to investigating. That nigga could change his lock code on his phone every day and I could still get into it. My mom always did say I should've gone to school for forensics or some shit, but I became a stripper instead. I hacked into his phone and any and everything he did with it came straight to my computer. That's how I found out where his little bitch got her nails done and where and when. I spend days and nights going through all of his text messages. He sweet talked this bitch like he never did me. So many times, he offered her money and she only refused. Yea he gave me money but only when I fucked him, just on some just because shit,

LA was even talking to his mama about her. This bitch had to be eliminated as I had a plan to befriend her and get into her head about LA. When I met her at the nail shop, she seemed like a weak bitch anyway so this would be an easy task. Trust, I was going to get LA one way or another, he just needed to see how down I was for him.

When he and I first met, he came to the club that I danced at every Thursday and would throw me hundreds of dollars. He tried to get at me numerous times, but I was fucking with this dude named Big C, so I had no love for him and turned him down time after time. Six months later Big C got fifteen years in jail for armed robbery and my pockets started to go a

TESHERA C.

little dry. Big C had offered me a lavish lifestyle, something that stripping alone couldn't do. That is when I set my eyes on LA, but he had changed and he wasn't into chasing bitches, the bitches chased him. They literally would follow him when he came to the club and pretty soon, he had fuck every last one of them even some of them together. I shot my shot but too bad he was with the bitch Jania. I solved that problem though and ran her ass off to down south somewhere. I knew something about the bitch that could have her killed, but I keep will that between us.

Finally, LA gave me a chance, but he was so bitter from Jania up and disappearing that he couldn't give me anything. It wasn't even about the money anymore, I genuinely liked this man, so I settled for late night booty calls and him throwing me a few hundred every now and them. Now things had to change, I am with child and I want my family. His lil' bitch can get ready to step willingly or get knocked the fuck off, her choice.

MOCHA

My life had become so mundane that I literally would go from home to work and back home again. Peaches tried getting me out of the house at times but most of the time I just wasn't feeling it. I had finally gotten LA out of my mind but for some reason my mood seemed forever gloomy. I hadn't talked to Pisces either, she was low, I guess shacked up with Zoe.

I was getting dressed for work, it was actually my day off, but I was going in for OT. What had my life became when I was happy to go to work on an off day. I peeped out of the window and saw that it was pouring down raining and I had just got my damn hair done. Now I was dreading going to work. I wrapped my hair up and then searched for my umbrella until I found it to be broken. Unable to shield myself from the rain I made a dash for it to my car.

I made it to the hospital and hour later thanks to the heavy traffic and two car accidents. The rain was pouring even harder now, and it was thundering out. I put my things away in my locker and as I was going to check my patients, I ran slam into my coworker Sheena.

"Hey girl," I greeted her.

"Hey, you didn't get my messages?"

I looked down and my phone was dead. "No, my phone is dead."

"Girl I was calling you to see if you could come in earlier, the ER is packed, and we just got a mass shooting that came in. About six guys came in here with fatal wounds, they say it was something to do with a gang, but girl we going to have a lot on our hands tonight and you may have to take a few more patients."

"Ok, that's fine. I will get right to it." I went to get my patients clipboards and I read the first name Lorenzo Green. I made my way up to the designated room and walked in to a man trying to remove his hospital band. "Excuse me sir, you don't need to do that," I said finally coming face to face with him.

"Mocha?" he called out, as if he were trying to figure out my name.

"It's nurse Hart."

"Mocha, it's me Zoe, LA peoples," I had only seen Zoe one time and that was at the club two months ago but now the face looked familiar. I rushed to him like he was my peoples.

"What are you doing here?" I asked, checking his charts to make sure he wasn't dying or something. Good thing he only had a flesh wood.

"I'm good, some shit popped off earlier. Ain't no big thing."

"What do you mean it's not a big thing, you're sitting here shot," my words then drifted off as I thought about LA. I could bet that his wild ass was right with Zoe when he got shot. My heart crashed to my feet, I had to make sure that LA was okay. I mean we weren't seeing eye to eye, but I would never wish for him to get shot. Zoe must've read my eyes, "He's here too. IDK how he doing, but he here," he said solemnly.

"Okay, I'm going to get this glass out of your arm and then I will check on him," Zoe whined like a bitch as I carefully took out the shards of glass that were in his arm. A bullet must've ricocheted from glass, then causing the glass to cut him. I tried probing Zoe on what happened, but he wouldn't say much, and it was irritating my soul. I finished up with him about forty minutes later and gave him percs and told him to stay put. I knew that he would try to leave the hospital against the doctor's wishes.

I checked the surgery schedule and learned that LA was currently undergoing surgery for a bullet that was lodged in his abdomen. I busied myself to keep from thinking about him, but nothing worked so I crashed in an empty room and just cried. I couldn't handle stuff like this. He told me he would be safe but who am I kidding, LA would die for his set and that was why we couldn't be together. I wasn't going to be burying him after he got himself into some mess.

I felt myself getting heated, so I wiped my tears and get myself together, I had other patients other than LA to worry about. If he wanted to bang and get himself killed, then that was his problem.

The ER was finally winding down and I needed to rest. I had come to the hospital at seven pm and it was now two am and I hadn't sat down yet. On my way to the café, I couldn't help but check to see if LA was out of surgery and indeed, he was. I ignored my hunger pains and the nursing of my feet so that I could just check on him. I got to his room, almost afraid to go in. What if he put me out? Or what if he didn't want to see me? Tons of questions were forming in my head, but I put them aside and entered the room. He was sleeping and probably knocked out from the surgery. I read his charts to see that he had been shot three times, once in the abdomen, and twice in the leg. His surgery went well, and he would be okay with some therapy.

I stared at him in his sleep almost wanting to smack him for scaring me to death. This lasted for about ten minutes before his eyes popped open. Shit scared me as I jumped back.

"Damn, I had to get shot and come to the hospital to see you huh?" he asked while trying to clear his throat. I poured his water from the pitcher sitting beside him "This is not the time to play," I said seriously.

"Sometimes you got to laugh to keep from crying," he replied.

Silence

"You don't have to stare at me like that. I'm not dead, ain't you supposed to be checking my vitals or some shit?"

He was actually right as I checked his vitals and blood pressure. I still didn't know what to say to him and then I just said fuck it "You know you could've got yourself killed tonight. I don't know what happed, but I know some mischief was involved. When are you going to slow down?"

"Why you care? Last time I talked to you; you wished my dick fell off."

"And the last time I talked to you, you weren't considering my feeling and thought that I was just supposed to believe your words without any actions behind them, but that's not the point-"

"That is the point, you have a problem with me, so let's talk it out face to face right now."

"I don't want to talk about that."

"Well I do. I never fucked or fucked with your cousin. I was hanging with Fo and nem one day and he bought some bitch to the crib. It was his girl and your cousin. She thought we was on some double date shit, but I wasn't feeling it. She tried to fuck me but I deaded that and ever since then she been on my dick. Me and that girl was never anything Mo."

Silence

"Don't get quiet now, this is what you wanted so what do you have to say now?"

I honestly didn't know what to say. "So, am I supposed to believe you over my cousin?"

"Hell yeah, yo' peoples get around. Why would she fuck with Zoe if we so called had a relationship?" he did have a point there and I never considered it.

Come here Mo?" he called out to me and I only shook my head no. I felt so stupid. "Please," he said nicely.

I walked over to him and he grabbed my hand. "I want to assure you right now that I would never put you in a position to have you out here looking dumb as long as you don't have me looking dumb. Let's work this shit out pretty girl."

That made me smile as he pulled me down on to the bed with him. "LA, be careful, you just got shot, and I don't want to hurt you."

"Girl, yo lil ass can hurt me. I'ma gangster," he said, seriously. I leaned in and kissed him. It was magical as I started to tingle all over.

"Aye can you do me something? He asked breaking our kiss. "Yea, what's up?"

"Go home and get naked and make a video for me I want you to get nasty with it." I laughed at his frankness cause he was dead serious, and his manhood was rising.

"Whelp, that's my cue. I have other patient to check out, piece out," I joked and left the room before I ended up getting fired for screwing a patient.

ZOE

"Throw that shit back," I demanded. I had finally got Ashlyn where I wanted her and that was in my bed and on my dick. She had called me over, a clown that she found out was married and I used that shit to my advantage. She was all vulnerable and shit, so I tried my hand and what do you know----- she went for it. We had been fucking like rabbits for day, me with a bullet wound and all.

She fussed my ass out for being irresponsible and getting shot and then we fucked, she picked her kid from school we fucked, she cooked a nigga a meal we fucked. Ya'll get the drill right. The only thing that was bothering me was the secret shit that she was on. I don't know about her, but I wasn't scared of LA, we were brothers, so I knew she probably was over reacting.

"Ahh!" she screamed out as I smacked her ass from the back. She was throwing it back and I damn sure was catching it. "Who pussy is this?" I asked while smacking that ass again.

Silence

Smack went the sound of my hand connecting to her ass again since she didn't wanna listen," I said, what is my name?" She still wouldn't budge until I yanked her back by her hair up to me. I whispered in her ear. "Say my name Ash," all that was her was out panting as I fondled her clit while pumping into her back side. I put my hands around her throat and added a little pressure but not enough to make her think I was trying to choke her out. "Say my name," I said again before putting more pressure on her neck.

Good girl Ash loved that shit as she moaned even louder screaming, "Lorenzo! Lorenzo!" Next, I was dumping all in her shit.

"Oh my god Zoe, I told you to pull out. You stay doing that. I don't know how many plan b pills I'ma have to take messing with you," she whined.

"You better not be taking no plan B pills," I threatened.

"Whatever, Zoe," she said while swaying her naked ass to the bathroom. Ashlyn was a petite girl, but she definitely could take pipe. We were exact opposite. I was tall and solid while she was 4'11" and weighed no more than a buck ten.

"So, I guess that we can announce our relationship at CJ's annual cookout Ash!" I yelled to the bathroom.

"Zoe, we aren't announcing anything because there is nothing to tell," *here she go with that shit.*

"Yo, you are tripping, you ain't gone keep hiding me like I'm a fuck nigga or something," I was now in the bathroom while she was sitting on the toilet.

"Can I get some privacy please?"

"Hell no, ain't no privacy."

"Zoe, we been having sex for two weeks and now you want to jump into a relationship?"

"Hell yeah, you know I wanted you since back in the day, but you said that I was too young, and you got with Sco. I wanted you before I even knew you, so yeah, I want a relationship. Me just fucking you doesn't suffice.

"Well it's going to have to suffice. Never mind that you're my brother-in-law's best friend, but you still in that gang shit and I don't have time for it."

"Aite bro. Well I'm good on you too then," I said, getting up off the bathroom floor to leave.

"Oh, so I'm your bro now."

CUFFED BY A GANGSTA: LA & MOCHA

I ignored her ass and got dressed and then she appeared from the bathroom looking sad. "Yo, you did this shit Ash."

"I know but I just have one request before you go."

"What man?"

She only looked like she had something she wanted to say but was scared. "Spit the shit out Ashlyn!"

"Okay, okay, can I get one more sample before you go?"

This girl had the audacity. I was now convinced that she only used me for my dick. I was okay with being a man whore, but not with Ashlyn. With her I wanted something real. "Nah, ah you ain't getting no more daddy dick until you act right. No more daddy dick for you."

She only pouted as she watched me leave. I ain't have time for that shit though. If Ashlyn didn't want my ass I would just have to settle for Pisces.

LA

"You think that you are so tough trying to walk without those crutches, but I bet you be hurting by the end of the night," Mocha said, while grilling my ass. She just couldn't leave the nurse shit at work and had been on my ass since I got out of the hospital a week ago.

"Mo, I have one living parent and she's at home somewhere," I responded back.

"Yeah okay, whatever grumpy," she said, stomping out of the room with her prissy ass. I was a little on edge today because it was the day of the cookout for CJ and I couldn't be on top of shit because I was limping. CJ's party was the most talked about event of the year and I couldn't let him down on his day. Fr, everything was pretty much done, and whatever wasn't the rest of the gang would handle it, I was just tripping.

"Babe what do you think about this dress?" Mocha asked, holding up some colorful shit. I just shook my head cause I didn't care what she wore. "Oh, and I meant to tell you that my friend will be meeting us at the cookout," she said nonchalantly.

"What friend? You don't have any friends."

"Correction. I didn't used to have friends, but I met this cool chick at the nail shop, and we've been hanging out a little."

"Oh, how come haven't met her?"

"You're going to meet her today silly," she said, and then pranced out of the room. When she came back, she was dressed form head to toe in the same colorful dress that she asked me if I liked. Her hair flowed freely on her shoulder and her face was just as pretty as the day that she had re-entered into my life.

"Let me help you with that," she said as she saw me struggling to get my pants on.

"I don't need your help Mo," she just stood there and watched me.

"What is up with you today? I hope you fix your attitude before you get out here in front of all of these people. Today is not about you. Remember that." With that she left the room.

We got to the cookout around four pm and it was jammed packed. We had rented out a huge field and when I say every square inch was packed, that's how many people came out to show love. As soon as I popped on the scene, niggas and bitches was walking up to me dapping me. The entire NHG gang wore green bandanas which was my favorite color. Moms had even showed up and looked to be having a good time and for the first time of the day a smile crept on my face.

MOCHA

I had never been to an event of someone that was of this magnitude before. The entire hood came out for CJ and for one there wasn't any drama just black folk getting along. Peaches texted me and told me that she was parking, so I decided to go and meet her. She had really shown out for the event as she wore Daisy dukes, a halter top and platinum blonde bundles in her hair. Honey was trying to snag a man tonight and she reminded me so much of Pisces who was also on her way.

"What's up girl?" I said, as I greeted her.

"Hey girl, I see it's popping out here," she said pulling her shorts up even higher exposing the cherry tattoo on her booty.

"Yea, it's a very nice turnout. I wish I would've met him."

"Oh yeah girl he was mad cool."

"Oh, you knew him. I thought you said you wasn't from here."

"I'm not, but in this small town and I was talking to a someone from the gang."

We walked into the gates of the cookout and Peaches immediately scanned the crowd. "You looking for someone?" I asked.

"No girl just thought I saw someone that I knew, but where yo man at I can't wait to meet him," she smiled.

"I'm surprised you don't know him, but it will not be hard to spot him. He is probably the only person hear sporting crutches."

I looked for LA and spotted him standing with a few of his friends and his mom who I had met when she came to the hospital to visit him.

"There he is, c'mon girl. I will introduce you two. Maybe he can put you in with his friend Nuke." The entire way walking over Peaches held her compact out and adjusted her outfit which made me kinda self-conscious. I hoped that I looked okay in my oversized highlighter dress and sandals. On our way over, a dude grabbed my hand and tried talking to me. I smiled politely and kept it moving but now before I heard another dude say "Bro, don't you know that's LA's girl. You don't want them kind of problems." I laughed to myself how my man's name rung bells, but I noticed that Peaches was frowning a bit.

"You okay girl?" I asked.

"Yeah I'm good," she said, with a smile. When we finally made it over to LA, he and the guys were laughing about something. He reached his arms out for me but all of a sudden turned stone cold.

"Babe, this is my friend Peaches that I've been telling you about."

"Hey Lance, nice to meet you. I've heard so much about you," Peaches said, while extending her hand. I didn't remember giving her LA real name, but I didn't think too much of it.

"Babe, say hi," I urged him as he stood there, but I couldn't read his face.

"What's up," he said dryly.

"It's very nice to meet you, hopefully we all can hang out sometime."

"Yeah girl, he has plenty of friends," I managed to get out before LA whisked me away.

"LA, what's wrong? That was so rude," I said, when we were out of ears reach.

"Yo, how you know that broad?"

"I told you we met at the nail shop. Why?"

"Because Mocha, you can't be so damn trusting of people that you barely know."

"LA, just in case you didn't know, I'm grown and more than capable of choosing who I want to be in my life."

"Man, you don't have to do all of that. I'm just looking out for you."

67

"Okay, well, I can look out for myself."

"Are you serious Mocha? You really bouta cop an attitude over that bitch. Damn ya'll must be friends, friends!"

"Look, I don't want to argue with you."

"Me either so give me a kiss," he demanded.

"Alright, ya'll break this shit up," LA's friend Nuke said breaking up our little moment. "Look who just walked in arm and arm."

ASHLYN

I had finally agreed to Zoe's terms of letting LA know that we were together the butterflies danced in my stomach as we entered the cookout and it seemed like all eyes were on us. We walked in arm and arm as Zoe brushed his hair with a random brush that he pulled out of his pocket. I could tell that he was a little nervous.

"Zoe, are you sure that you want to do this?"

"Man, we here now. Its already done."

We walked over to where the crew was and not a word was spoken only mean glares. I knew I shouldn't have gone through with this shit. These niggas loved Roscoe and would never forgive me for getting with his brother's friend.

"Hell going on here?" LA was the first to speak up like always. "And where my niece at?" he grilled me.

"She's with my mom LA, how are you?"

"I'm good sis, what about you and Zoe? What, ya'll got here at the same time or something?"

"Nah, bruh we came her together." Zoe held his hand out for some dap, but LA only looked at him as if he had a disease or something.

"Man, why the fuck both of ya'll looking so dumb. If ya'll got some shit to say, spit it out. Ya'll came in here all chummy together. What's good?"

"Me and Ashlyn are together. There I said it," Zoe said, as if he was happy to get that off of his chest.

"Damn that's how you rocking Ash, out of all the niggas?"

"Look LA it's not even like that-" I started but LA cut me out with the wave of his hand.

"You're the mother of my niece so I won't disrespect you, but I also don't want nothing to do with yo ass either, you or this lame ass nigga here," he said pointing at Zoe.

"LA don't be like that..."

"Nah, baby don't beg him to accept us, this something he just gone have to get used to," Zoe said confidently.

"Nigga, I don't have to get used to shit. Fuck you think you talking to?" LA said while reaching for his waist. A couple of the guys got in between them to calm everything down and I all of a sudden regretted my decision to be with Zoe, I didn't want any wars started over me.

"C'mon man, ya'll better than that," a guy spoke. We all NHG."

"Man, this nigga ain't NHG, fucking Sco, bm. This nigga ain't with the gang no more."

"Says who nigga, the bylaws stated that it's a group vote to kick somebody out, so if you want me out, set up a meeting so we all can vote. Until them I'm NHG!"

Zoe grabbed my hand and then we left. I wanted to stay and talk to LA, but I would be so disrespectful to Zoe, he had stood up for our relationship and for that I would always respect him.

MOCHA

LA drove home with fury in his eyes and for some reason the stress and frustration that he was feeling was starting to rub off on me. We couldn't even enjoy the remainder of the cookout because LA was so upset and spazzing out on everyone. I had only heard the tail end of what happened between he and Zoe, but I dared to ask him the details. When we finally got to his house, there was still silence between us and it was scaring me. I honestly would have rather him to have taken me to my place since he was acting like he was alone anyway.

"Babe, can I get you anything?" I said breaking the silence, but I didn't get an answer. I decided to just leave him to himself and I went to heat up my plate that I had got from the cookout. I was starving and dusted the food off in a matter in minutes. When I went back upstairs, LA was finally sleeping, and I decided that I would join him.

LA

I must've fell asleep early as hell because when I woke back up it was three am and Mocha was nowhere in sight. I called out to her but got no answer, so I guessed that she went home. I went down stairs to get a drink and then made my way back to my room to go back to sleep when I heard a sound. I grabbed my gun and went toward the sound that was apparently coming from the guest bathroom. I opened the door slightly and I saw Mocha hovered over the toilet with a tooth brush down her throat making herself throw up,

"Yo, Mocha, what the fuck are you doing?" I said, yanking her up. There was vomit all around her mouth as she looked at me lazily.

"Fuck are you doing making yourself throw up?"

"I wasn't. I just don't feel good," she cried.

"So, you make yourself throw the fuck up cause you don't feel good?" I asked seriously.

"I don't know," she answered, which confused the hell out of me. I looked into her eyes and for the first time since I had met her, I saw that she had problems too. I held her in my arms for a moment as she wept and then I put her in the shower. For the rest of the night no words were spoken until she drifted off. That night I didn't get any sleep just thinking about her and the shit with Zoe and Ashlyn. There was just too much shit going on.

The next day came and Mocha avoided me as she got ready to go to work. I decided that I would let her talk when she was ready because I had other shit to handle, first being Peaches hoe ass. I pulled up to her crib and looked under a flower pot for her extra key and just like I expected it was there. Predictable bitch. I opened the door to her filthy ass house. The bitch loved filling up her closet but wouldn't spend a dime of getting her fucking house in order. She had the same basic ass sectional that all the hood hoes got with their income tax check. She didn't even hear me come in as she ran the nigga pockets that was currently sleeping in her bed.

"You a dirty bitch, I see."

She peeked her head up surprised that I was in her presence.

"LA, baby what are you doing here," his voice full of fear.

"Bitch! I'm asking the questions. How the fuck did yo scheming ass meet my girl?"

"We go to the same nail shop."

"And it was just a coincidence that you start going to the same nail salon with my bitch?"

"Yes baby, now calm down and let me please you," she said reaching for my belt buckle."

I swatted her hand away and grabbed her by her neck. "Let me tell yo lil simple ass something. I don't know what kind of stunt you were trying to pull, but I will fucking kill you. Like literally kill you and dispose of your body. Don't ever in yo muthafucking life think you doing something to get at my girl cause at the end of the day you gone always lose when fucking with Mocha." I let her go and flung her ass on the bed all the while her dude stayed sleep. "And clean this damn pigsty up with you dirty ass." I walked out hoping that Peaches would not take my threats as idle because we both knew what I was capable of.

PISCES

I almost fell the fuck out when I learned that both of my niggas were now locked down by Mocha's basic ass and Ashlyn's hoe ass. I don't know what I was doing to be having so much bad luck but there was one thing that would keep me at the top spot. I was now pregnant, and I was one hundred and five percent sure that it was Zoe's baby. I knew that this would make LA never want me but at least my bag would be secured by being Lorenzo's baby mama. I already had names picked out and everything. If it was a boy, it would be a junior and if it was a girl, I would name her Zoey. Life would be great, but I would just have to get Ashlyn out of the damn picture.

    I decided to call my cousin up because she was a little MIA lately and I wanted to be a little nosey about what was going on between her and LA. I called her once and it went straight to voicemail, so I called her right back and the bitch answered.

    "Hello, she said softy," I hinted some sadness in her voice.

    "What's up cousin? Haven't heard from your gone ass. What is good?"

    "Girl I am fine, but I try to stay away from your negativity. I already have too much shit going on in my life and don't need the extra.

    "Cousin you know, I be tripping sometimes but wats going on. You know I'm always here for you.

"Girl I don't know. I guess LA and I have hit sort of a rough patch I hardly see him anymore and when we are together, he is so angry over that Zoe and Ashlyn shit.

"Damn for real? That is messed up for Ashlyn to mess with her dead baby daddy friend.

"Girls it's all too much, but I'm hanging in there."

"Well girl what are you doing for your birthday?"

Silence

Mocha stalled for a but so I knew that the dumb bitch had forget her own birthday.

"I really don't want to do anything," she answered.

"What? You're turning twenty-five. We need to do something. Let me plan a dinner or something for you."

"I don't know P."

"Girl come on, you deserve it," I lied.

"Okay, girl but nothing too big, small and intimate."

"Okay, I got you and I will call you with the details."

I hung up the phone with a smile on my face because I would definitely be inviting someone to the party that Mocha would never fucking expect. It would be a night of surprises.

MOCHA

I couldn't believe that I had almost forgot that my birthday was coming up. I would be twenty-four on May twenty-third. So much shit had been going on that I was lacking on self-care and worrying about LA's ass wasn't helping. He had asked me to come to his house and here he was ignoring me and leaving me most of the time. I wondered if we would last much longer. I stepped out of the bathroom from my phone call with P and bumped slam into LA.

"Why you whispering in the bathroom?" he asked.

"I wasn't whispering," I said, trying to walk past him, but he grabbed my arm.

"Did I hear you say that your birthday is coming up?"

"Were you ease dropping on my conversation?"

"Yeah kinda, but for real babe, is your birthday coming up? Why didn't you tell me?"

"Because lately you've been in your own world and I didn't want to disturb you," he rested his head in his hands before pulling me towards the couch.

"Look babe, I know I been a little distant lately, but don't ever think that I would miss a special day like your birthday," he said sincerely.

"So, why have you been shutting me out lately?"

"It's not like I was doing it on purpose but this shit with Zoe and Ash, really been bugging me and learning that you are bulimic through me for a loop to."

"Well, I'm better now, but what is your real problem with it? Zoe came along after your brother so it not like he's breaking some kind of bro code and Zoe is someone that you would trust with your life. Why wouldn't you want Ashlyn with someone like that?"

LA looked at me for a while before finally nodding his head. "You right babe, I should've been talked to you instead of being a dick head."

"Yes, dickhead, next time let me in." From the hungry look in his eyes, I knew what was about to go down as he wasted no time, ripping my dress off of me and buried his face in my pussy. He was licking and slurping for dear life as my juices dripped from his chin, sounded like stomping in rain puddles. He then flipped me over and spread my cheeks wide, before I felt his wet tongue in my ass hole. This was a first for me, so it took a little time for me to get used to the feeling. He went up and down with his tongue as he licked my ass crack clean. "Oh yes, LA," I moaned.

Slap! The stinging on my ass mad me yelp in pain "What I tell you about calling me that?" he entered me from the back ramming all ten inched inside of me. I yelped out in ecstasy as his long strokes were felt in my stomach. It wasn't long before we both came and it seemed that out of the blue, we were both happy again.

LA

It was time for our monthly meeting as I reflected on the little piece of advice that Mocha gave me. She did make sense, but I was still mad. It just seemed like some snake shit and the whole time they were sneaking around behind my back because they knew that the shit was wrong. I walked into the warehouse wearing a scowl. I was just ready to discuss our business and get back home to my girl. I was greeted by daps and head nods as I started the meeting discussing numbers and upcoming plans to open another chop shop. Once the meeting was over, I made my way out but was stopped by Zoe with a pitiful look on his face. "Yo bro, this how we carry it now?"

"Zoe, the only reason I didn't bring this shit to a vote is because I know that you're a valuable asset to the team and as far as you and Ashlyn, I can't even hate on what ya'll have, but at the same time I don't move how you move, so I don't want anything to do with either of you. There is no beef, just don't cross my path. I then walked away leaving him standing there.

MOCHA

I dragged my feet across the parking lot as I was dead ass tired from working a double. You could tell when it was warm outside because we had more gunshot victims then a little bit. I had nursed at least four different wounds during my shift and the shit was kinda depressing. I drove home half-awake wondering how I had even made it. My eyes were literally shutting as I walked through my door, but they were immediately opened when I saw my living room floor covered in white roses and big balloons that read out twenty-five. I followed the trail of roses up to my bed room where there was a rack of clothing waiting for me and several name branded shoes in boxes on the floor. The rack had to have had at least $10,000 worth of clothing on it as I fumbled through the expensive price tags.

What I saw next made me want to go grab a damn fur coat or something. On my dresser sat six boxes filled with ice along with the words 'pick one' balloons floated in the air. I was literally blinded by the six rings that sat in front of me and I wondered if LA was about to propose. My anxiety started to kick in and I felt beads of sweat forming on my brow. As if he was reading my thoughts. LA appeared in the room and swooped me into his arms.

"Happy birthday baby," he said while embracing me.

"Lance..." I called out; eyes filled with tears. "You didn't have to do all of this. I stood there speechless, wondering if I was deserving of all of this. It wasn't even about the money but more so the thought that he had put into everything.

"Stop crying punk. You know I had to go all out for my baby's birthday. The last few months that you been in my life has been nothing short of paradise, so I wanted to show my appreciation.

My heart beat rapidly through my chest as I expected LA to pop the question from how deep he was being. I even held out my hand slightly.

LA chucked just a bit before speaking "Mocha you know I'm feeling the hell out of you, but this isn't a proposal baby girl." I immediately yanked my hand back a bit embarrassed.

"Don't be like that," LA said, grabbing me by my waist. "Just give me a lil' while and you will have that ring finger iced out, now go over there and tell me which promise ring you want. After staring at the rings like a little girl at a candy store, I finally picked a 1.35 carat emerald cut ring in 14k white gold. The damn thing weighed a ton, but it was oh so pretty.

"Thank you for everything babe," I said still glancing at my ring that fit my finger perfectly.

"Don't think me yet, I'm not done." Then pulled out a map and I was confused as hell.

"Fix your face," he said, while laughing and then tying a blind fold around my eyes. He thing spun me around several times and then told me to put one finger anywhere on the map. I was dizzy as hell probably not going anywhere near the map when he led me a little. I place my hand on the map and then LA removed the blindfold. When I looked down my hand was on Maldives.

"Guess, we going to Bali babe."

"What LA?" I asked a little confused.

"I'm booking us a flight to Bali for the in a few months. You coming or going?" he joked.

"Hell yeah, I'm going. Oh my god, this has been the best birthday ever. I don't know how I'm going to top this when yours comes around," I joked.

"Well, yo ass better get to thinking," he said, still holding me in his arms. So far, my day was going perfectly.

"Surprise!" everyone yelled out as I entered the private room that my birthday dinner would be held at. I knew that P was planning a little shin dig for me but what I didn't know is that she had invited my parents. It had been almost a year since I had seen them and who knew that they would come from Virginia just for my birthday.

"Well look at you young lady," my mom said pinching my cheeks and hugging me followed by a tight bear hug from my father. Other than my parents, Ashlyn, P's mom and sister and a few of my work associates had all shown up and I was pleased to say the least. The next person that I saw really took me by surprise and not in a good way. In walked Keen, my ex-boyfriend who had played me like a damn fiddle for the two years that we were together. He scrolled in with a bouquet of white roses and walked right up to me and pecked me on the cheek like LA wasn't even there.

"Kenny what are you doing here?" I managed to say. I was acting like I had been caught cheating or something when I hadn't seen this corny dude in a year.

"Yo bruh, fuck are you?" LA butted in grabbing my arm.

"I'm Kenneth and you are?" Kenny sad reaching his hand out to shake. LA looked at his hand like it stink.

"Aite Kenneth well keep your hands to your damn self."

"I'm sorry, who are you again?" Kenny was really trying it and when I saw that one vein appear on LA's forehead, I knew it wouldn't be long before he snapped.

"Babe, come on let's sit down," I said practically pulling LA, while he mean mugged Kenny.

"Babe? Pisces, I thought you told me that she was single?" Kenny said, now facing P with a perplexed stare.

"Shit, I thought she was," P lied. "I mean I knew that she was dating but I didn't know she was taking anyone seriously," her tone was laced with envy and at this point I could've smacked the bitch.

"Oh damn, well I will go. I won't stay anywhere where I'm not welcomed."

"Yeah, step bro," LA spoke forcefully while everyone else in the room watched on. Kenneth left but not before sneakily winking at me and the mood was so thrown off. LA wouldn't even talk to me like the shit was my fault or something. My mom tried to lighten the mood by starting a conversation but while everyone talked LA only stared in his phone, so freaking embarrassing. I decided to text him so everyone wouldn't be up in our business.

Me: Fix your attitude.

LA: Fuck you!

Me: What is your problem? I didn't know that he would be here.

LA: And you acted like you didn't mind the shit either.

Me: You're being very childish right now and if you're going to continue to sit here just looking stupid, maybe you should leave.

LA: You don't have to tell me twice. Weak ass dinner.

LA got up to excuse himself from the table and my heart sank. Like he was actually going to leave me on my birthday over some bullshit. Just as he was leaving, I was met with another familiar face.

"Momo!" my big brother Yahseem called out me. My brother had just got out of jail after doing a five-year bid and since he had been home for the last four months, I hadn't seen him, we had only spoken on the phone. I jumped up out of my seat and hugged him tightly. The nigga was big as hell over my 5'3" frame. LA only stood staring at us and I know that he was still tripping because I had told him plenty of times about my older brother Yahseem. It wasn't until he let me go that I saw exactly what LA was staring at. There in big black bold letter across his forearm read NGK or die. My birthday was slowly turning into a damn shit show.

The two then both started staring at one another with vengeance in their eyes. "Damn sis, you didn't tell me that you was dating a bitch ass NHG nigga."

"Nigga I'm not gone bust yo ass in front of your people, but I suggest you watch how you talk to me."

"Now look," my dad finally interrupted. "Ya'll not about to bring this gang shit up in here on my baby's birthday. Take that shit to the streets."

"Yeah you right pops. I'ma let ya'll enjoy ya'll lil moment though. I will catch you in traffic gang," LA said before walking off and I was right on his heels.

"LA, wait where are you going?" I yelled, once we were outside.

"Fuck you think I'm going? Away from yo ass!" I was stunned at the way that he was talking to me. I hadn't done anything to him. "So why are you mad at me though? I'm confused.

"You must be slow. First yo weird ass ex come to your party and ya'll had some hit going on and then yo beefy ass brother come in on some shit. You ain't telling me that you didn't know that that nigga was riding with NBK."

"I didn't know! Why in the hell would I have even given you the time of day if my brother was in a rival gang? You sound stupid as hell."

"Man, I'm not trying to hear all of that," he waved me off. While steadily walking away.

"Stop walking away from me Lance. What about us? You just gone give up on us over some childish gang shit?"

"What do you expect me to do Mocha?"

"Grow the fuck up, that's what!"

"Man, I'm not doing this with you. I'm gone!" I wasn't going to continue to chase him or beg him to be with me, so I let him go. Even though it felt like my heart was breaking into a million pieces, if he wanted to leave, I would let him.

ASHLYN

I scooped Ross up from the sitters as I explained the wreck of a dinner that Mocha invited me to. I know she didn't expect for all of that to go down and I actually felt bad for the poor girl. Imagine having your bother and mans at odds with one another wanting to blow each other brains out.

"So, you telling me that Mocha's brother is NBK and she didn't know."

"Yes Zoe, she was totally shocked when it all went down. You can't fake the surprise."

"Damn I know LA wanted to smoke both of their asses."

"He was mad as hell, but you can tell that he really likes that girl. I wish that he could just get over his bullshit ass ego. Is he still not talking to you?"

"Man, you know that nigga stubborn as hell. He will come around eventually."

"I hope so, but anyways, where you at and when you coming on this side?"

"I'm out making moves love. I will be in a little late tonight."

"How late?"

"Twelve or one," I looked at the phone as if he had lost his mind.

"You must be going to your house because you are not walking up in my home that late disturbing my daughter and I."

"Girl boo. I will be over there in bout an hour with your spoiled ass."

"Yeah you better be," I laughed.

"Nah, but for real though, I been thinking bout a lot of shit lately and I think I'm ready to let NHG go. Too many niggas dropping like flies and I'm not trying to go that route, I gotta be here for my three girls."

"Girls?" I questioned putting an emphasis on the "s".

"Yeah, you, Ross the boss and shorty duwop in your stomach."

"Boy you are crazy! I am not pregnant."

"Aite, wait and see. I been putting in overtime in that pussy, so I know."

"Boy you are cra-" I was cut off by the spraying sound of bullets on the other end of the phone and then screeching tires.

"Baby!" I yelled out but got no response. "Zoe if you can hear me please say something!" I yelled fearing for the worst.

I called out Zoe's name for what seemed like forever until the line was disconnected.

MOCHA

It had been a few days since I had talked to LA and I was going crazy. He wasn't answering my calls and he went on as if what we had never meant anything to him. On day four, I was fed the fuckup and decided to pay him a visit. I thought that he would be changed the locks on me but surprisingly he didn't, and I waltzed right on in.

His home was clean as usual, but I knew exactly what he was doing when I heard music coming from the third level of the house. He was in his makeshift gym. I went to where he was, and he was laid out on the weight bench lifting weights. I admired the glistening sweat that ran down his six pack as his package bulged beneath his grey sweats. Boy it was a sight to see considering that I hadn't had one drop of him because he was mad at me.

I stood there in a daze when he suddenly lifted himself up and looked at me. It was like he could feel my presence or something like I always felt his. He wiped his brow before catching his breath and finally addressing me.

"Mo what are you doing here?" he asked calmly.

"I came here to talk," I answered lowly. "Why have you been ignoring me?

"Mo, you know how this shit go."

"What shit? You mean my brother being down with NBK? Because that has nothing to do with us."

"What Mo? You can't be that damn blonde. If I killed your fucking brother, then would it have something to do with us?" he asked giving me an intense stare.

"Don't say that. It doesn't even have to come to that."

"So, what the fuck does it have to come to then? Huh? You now I'm NHG till I die and I'm not letting up anytime soon."

"And that's your damn problem! You're so obsessed with getting get back for you dead brother that you can't even live your own life."

"My dead brother?" he repeated, like he was trying to understand what I had just said.

"You know I didn't mean it like that, and I would never disrespect him but-"

"Ain't no fucking but's. You and yo brother OOP and for that I can't fuck with you." The tears started to roll down my eyes and LA looked away from me like my pain meant nothing to him.

"So, this is it?" I said, wiping my face. "This is how you're going to do me after I let down every wall that I had for you. I even lowered my standards for you, and you sit here and act like we, us, never meant anything to you. I hope the gang life brings you everything that you need, and I especially pray that your fate doesn't end up like your brothers." With that, I wiped my last tear and left LA with a heart split in two.

I drove home trying to get LA out of my head, but it didn't work but now I wasn't sad, but angry as hell. LA was what one considered a fuck nigga, who wouldn't know a good girl if she hit him dead in the face. After work and that conversation that I had just had with him all I wanted to do was shower and crash. I needed to drown out all of the confusion in my head. Guess we were not going to Bali anymore.

My plans were quickly changed as I walked into my house to see my brother and four of his friends, I didn't even have to guess that they were NBK before I saw the three letters tattooed on each of their faces. My house was smoked out as hell, music blasting and one dude even had his feet propped up on my damn ottoman. This is not what I was prepared for when I agreed to let my brother crash with me until he got his own apartment.

"Yo, what up sis?" Yahseem greeted me turning the music down.

"What is up with you and these random men in my house?"

"Oh sis, these my niggas, Dre, Slim, Tone and Ree," they each nodded at me but Slim's eyes lingered a little too long on my ass in these blue scrubs.

"Well, it's time for your company to go. I'm tired and just want to relax in my home alone."

"Damn Mo! You must've had a bad day or something."

"Yeah so what, I expect my house to be empty in the next five minutes."

"Shawty you ain't gotta tell me twice," Tone said before getting up and leaving, the other two followed suit, but slim stayed.

"I won't looking at yo ass a few minutes ago, I was looking at the that damn whole in them shits. You might want to trash those. It's not attractive. You cute though," he said walking by me and out of the house. Yahseem then came out of the kitchen and went with them letting me know that he would be homes later. I couldn't believe the audacity of his friend, but he was a little cute with those stone-gray eyes and stone demeaner. He could be just the little distraction to get me over the donkey of the day LA.

I woke up the next afternoon feeling like a brand-new woman as I had slept the entire night and day away. The only reason that I had even gotten up was to release my bladder and see what was going on, on social media. My phone had been buzzing with notification all night, so I had to see what was up. More than likely it was somebody arguing over a dirty dog man or something like that.

I scrolled down my timeline and stopped suddenly when I saw a status that said, "Get well soon Zoe," there had to be a million and one Zoe's in the world, so I kept scrolling only to see about four more statuses saying the same thing. My suspicions were confirmed when someone used his real name and followed by NHG forever. I gasped as I also read that he had been shot five times and was in critical condition. My first instinct was to call and check on LA, but I decided against it. He and Zoe had been at odds lately, but I know that he was losing it right now. LA's two brothers were killed and now this. When would these men realize that the whole gang scene was not worth so many people losing their lives?

My thoughts automatically went to Ashlyn and I couldn't even imagine what she was going through right now. Zoe had just been in the hospital a month prior for getting shot and here he was again in a worse situation. NHG gang needed to be deaded and over with.

PISCES

When I heard that my baby daddy had been shot on the news my heart crashed to my feet. It was then when I realized just how much he meant to me. I was now eight weeks pregnant by Zoe and I prayed that he would make it through to meet our little one. I kept it on the hush hush for a while just to make sure that it was real.

I drove through the night like a bat out of hell to go and see Zoe. I had even taken my mom's car without her permission, but I really couldn't think about how she would react. After almost cussing a nurse out because she refused to let be back because I had forgot my ID, I was finally about five feet away from his room and my heart beat out of my chest. I said a silent prayer before going in and gently giggled the door knob. As soon as I entered the room I was met with a gloomy feeling. The light was dimly lit, and I almost broke down when I saw Zoe spread out on the bed hooked up to various tubes. I could hardly even see his face as there was a thick white tube coming from his mouth. I held his hand and it was ice cold and it came to me how much I really did care for him. Yeah, I was using him to get to LA at first but now that his kid was swimming inside of me, I felt more closer to him than ever.

I stared at him sadly when I heard the toilet flush from the bathroom. The water was quickly cut on and shut off before the door was opened.

Out came Ashlyn and she almost jumped out of her skin when she seen me. The next few seconds were filled with us exchanging evil glances.

"Can I help you?' she said, with her hand resting on her hip. She looked tired as the dark circles had begun to reside around her eyes on her cream-colored skin.

"Nah, I'm good," I said, quickly and then and then turned back around to face Zoe."

"Well I'm going to ask you one time nicely to leave before I have you escorted out."

"Bitch, you not his wife! You don't call the shots here. I will leave when I'm good and damn ready."

"You not gonna be satisfied until I smack the shit out of you huh? You have no place here. Zoe told me that ya'll was messing around but that's all it was sweetie. If he was up, he would tell you the same thing," she said smartly.

"And if he was up, he would also tell you this," I said lifting my jacket so that she could see my growing belly. "Yeah, that's right bitch, I'm pregnant. Pick your face up off of the ground." I could see the steam sprout from her ears as I smiled a devilish smile.

"Bitch, if we weren't in this hospital, I would beat your ass, but trust I will see you," she said, before grabbing her things and leaving. I couldn't believe her weak ass just left; bitch was weak as hell. I pulled a chair closer to Zoe and then placed my hand in his before peacefully falling asleep.

MOCHA

   I made my way home from yet another mundane day at the hospital. I was so ready for a vacation, so I planned to visit my family in Virginia just to get away from Philly for a while. My supervisor even hooked me up with privileges at Norfolk General Hospital for the time being. I planned to go home to start packing and book a rental so that I could drive out the next weekend.

 I walked in to my place being spotless. The air smelled of Fabuloso and Meek Mill blasted through my crib. I guess my brother was tired of me bitching and yelling every day, so he decided to finally clean up. I walked in the kitchen to see him rolling up at my kitchen table while Slim scrolled through his phone. They both looked up when they saw me and Rahkeem went to turn the music down. "What's up sis?" he greeted me.

 "Hey," I said, while looking through the fridge noticing that he had restocked the fried. "What's going on with you?" I asked, suspiciously. "You done cleaned up and bought food."

 "Damn Mo, ain't nothing up," he laughed.

 "He cleaned up because he was tired of yo' ass coming home with that damn scowl on you face," Slim commented.

 "I do not always have a scowl on my face. And who was even talking to you? Better yet, why are you always here?" I replied. This nigga was at my house at least three times a week. "Ya'll don't have a lil secret relationship that I don't know about do you?" I joked, and each of them mean mugged me.

"Nah, you must be getting us confused with that NHG nigga that you used to fuck with," Slim said.

I looked at my brother who smirked before walking off.

"Don't get quiet now," Slim said.

"Boy, I'm not paying you any attention," I said, pulling out fruit to make a fruit salad.

"Yeah, I know. But check this out. I need your expertise on something."

"On what?"

"I want to do something nice for my girl. She been pressing a nigga bout' getting married, so I need to get her something in the meantime to shut her up," here I was thinking that he was flirting with me and he had a whole girl that he wanted me to shop for.

"Why won't you just marry her?" I asked.

"I'm just not ready. I love her to death, but I still got some dog in me."

"Guys for you," I said, shaking my head. My thoughts immediately went to LA, who I hadn't spoken to in two weeks. He was just as much as a game player as Slim was.

"So, you gone help me out or nah?"

"Well what do you need me to do?"

"Let's slide out to the jewelry store."

"When? Now?"

"Yeah, I will wait for you to change out of them scrubs."

One hour later I was riding in the passenger seat of Slim's Audi as he bobbed his head to some old school Public Enemy. Slim was so damn fine and ink covered his pecan colored skin. He caught me smiling at him and he only smirked before we had finally made it to the jewelry store. We stayed in the jewelry store for thirty minutes and picked his girlfriend out a cute cannery diamond.

"Aye, I got one more place to go," he stated. "Fix your face. You don't have anything else to do but curl in the bed and watch some Lifetime or some shit," he joked when he saw my face.

"I don't even watch Lifetime," I lied.

When we made it to the mall, my nerves started to get the best of me. It was NHG stomping grounds as I had come to this specific mall with LA on more than one occasion. Slim was saying something about him having to pick up some shoes and when I said that I would just stay in the car, he basically lifted my ass out of the car and carried me into the mall. To passersby's, we probably looked like a couple playing, but I was actually fighting his ass and he liked it. He continued to steal quick glances of my ass as if we hadn't just left from shopping for his girlfriend.

We walked into the store and he was greeted like he was royalty or something. Everyone dapped him up and showed him love. He even introduced me as his peoples but winked his eye at a Jadakiss look-alike.

"Don't be introducing me to people," I said, once he had got his two pair of kicks and we were leaving the store.

"What was I supposed to do? You crazy man," he said laughing. I laughed a little too and pushed him because I did sound childish. My laugh was suddenly halted when I saw a smiling LA walking with some chick. I tried tearing my eyes from them but couldn't. He seemed really happy as the girl showed him something on her phone. While I was dying inside, LA was out not giving a damn about me. I ripped my eyes away from him but now before he looked dead at me and then to Slim. The look in his eyes was one that I had never seen before, it was hate mixed with fury.

I latched on to Slims arm and he noticed me shaking like a leaf and looked up from his phone. As if he could sense his enemies, he looked right up at LA.

"Yo, you scared of this nigga?" he asked.

"No, but I would just like to go," I said, with my voice shaking.

"Aye nigga, you see something you like over here?" Slim said to LA, totally ignoring my request.

"You a pussy boi! You want to pop shit here, cause you know you can't be touched. Fuck outta here!" LA spoke with his hand placed firmly on his waist.

"Pussy! Man, you crazy. You out here wining and dining bitches while yo mans is laid up in the hospital right now. Now that's pussy," Slim said placing his arm around my shoulder. I now felt like I was a paw in their little game. The two then drew their weapons and aimed at one another like they weren't in the middle of a damn mall. People were recording and everything and I'm sure mall security would soon be on their way with the boys in blue. I pled with LA with my eyes and mouthed to him *please don't*. For a moment it felt that he was wrapped in the trance of me as he stared intently with a little sadness in his eyes. He then walked away leaving the girl looking stupid. I looked at Slim and he had a never to be smiling. I stormed off and called a damn Uber. Slim's ass had better not ever come to my damn house again.

ASHLYN

I laid in my bed staring at the two trash bags that I had filled with Zoe's things. A part of me told me that I was over exaggerating but the other part of me said fuck him. How could he lay beside me every night and promise me all of these things about our future but be still dicking Pisces down. I did the math and Zoe and I had been a monogamous couple for about four months now, and the bitch didn't look like she was that far along.

The nerve of that dirty hoe marching into my man's room like she was the girlfriend when she was nothing more than a side hoe. I was getting upset just thinking about the shit. My kid had even grown to love Zoe and here I was choosing him over LA and the whole time he was still fucking P. Yeah, he had told be about them in the past, but he left out that the bitch was still hanging around. My phone rang and it was Mo. She and I had been talking more ever since she had invited me to her birthday. We both confided in one another about our hardheaded ass men and right now we were both going through it with their asses.

"Hello," I answered.

"Girl, what is wrong with you? I can hear it all in your voice," Mo said like she could read me through the phone or something.

"Girl, just thinking about the whole situation with your cousin and Zoe, you know the only reason I haven't tapped that ass yet is because of you."

"Girl trust me I know. I grew up with P's ass and she was always up to some conniving shit of doing something crazy. All while we were growing up, she would date guys that I liked behind my back and everything. It took me till now to realize that she is not loyal to anyone but herself."

"Wow, you wouldn't even think that ya'll are cousins. Ya'll definitely live by different standards of life."

"Yeah, it's crazy girl but enough about her. I have to tell you about the crap that went down at the mall today." Mo filled me in on the entire debacle with her LA and the NBK guy and I wasn't even shocked. I knew LA would flip if he ever caught her with an NBK nigga and wasn't even about the set life but more because he was in love with the girl. He could fake it all he wanted but I could see right through him.

"Girl, yo ass really went to the mall with an NBK?" I asked.

"Yes, it was not even like that. I was kinda iffy about it, but I thought that LA was over me."

"Well, have you talked to him since?"

"No, I'm scared to even try to talk to him. LA made it clear that he wanted nothing to do with me."

"Girl I think ya'll need to talk. He's a hothead but he is also a little softie on the inside."

"Girl look who's talking. You telling me to talk to LA, and you are ready to give up on Zoe, and you haven't even heard his side of the story yet."

"Girl, the story ended when the bitch said that she was pregnant. I loved Roscoe, god rest his soul to death, but he cheated on me throughout our entire damn relationship and then died on me. I will not go through that again with another man, not ever."

"Well I definitely understand that girl and I respect your choice," she replied when there was a beep on my line. I put Mocha on hold and answered it.

"Hello," I answered.

"Yo Ash."

"Who is this?"

"This Nuke," he replied excitedly.

"Oh hey, what's up?" I asked finally catching his voice. He was Zoe's cousin.

"Ash! Zoe is up! My mans is finally up!"

LA

I couldn't bring myself to go to the hospital to see Zoe because of my own selfish feeling but I made it my mission to avenge the hit that he had took. Zoe was laid up in a hospital bed with thirteen holes through his body while them NBK nigga was probably laughing at us.

I laced my Timbs and pulled my skully over my head as tonight would be one of many nights where death would roam the air. I didn't know if my plan would work and my anger was probably getting the best of me, but I really didn't give a fuck. If I had to die for my set I would. I crept through the night in a beat-up Chevy that I would never ever be caught dead in, but tonight was a must.

I arrived at a somewhat upscale neighborhood, where nice fancy cars aligned the streets. It was so crazy to me that niggas were out here living this lavish while their workers were in the hood pinching pennies. I parked the old Chevy in front of the home and walked up to the door balancing a pizza in one hand. I anxiously rang the doorbell as my trigger finger inched at the thought of what was about to happen. The door was swung open and I was met with Lou, the grandson of the NHG creator. NHG went back before I was born and now the younger niggas were running shit while their peoples were either dead or in jail.

"Pizza delivery," I said, while my Philly brim sat low over my eyes.

"Nigga we ain't order no pizza, but we will take it though," Lou joked while reaching out to grab the box. It was then that his eyes finally met with mine and before his instincts could kick in, it was too late. I flashed the pizza box open and grabbed the Glock that was inside of it. Before Lou could even call for help, bullet holes stung through his chest. He dropped instantly as I made my way through the home shooting anyone in sight. I had made sure to do my due diligence to make sure that no women or kids were home so I could focus on my target. When I got down to my last bullet, there lay the dead bodies of Lou, and two of his runners Stan and Lee. I quickly swept the house making sure it was empty and just as soon as I was in, I was out.

I left the old hooptie right where it was parked, careful to wear gloves the entire time. I swiftly walked to my car which was one block over and got the fuck out of dodge. I was content for now but, in due time there would be more bloodshed to come.

ASHLYN

I nervously paced the hallways outside of Zoe's hospital room as I went back and forth in my head about what to say to him. A part of me was happy that he was awake and good but the other part of me couldn't get the bitch Pisces from my head. I didn't know why I couldn't get her from off of my brain, but I couldn't top thinking about her and the bastard child that she was carrying.

I remember when I was about four months pregnant with Ross, some girl called herself coming to me woman to woman and telling me that Roscoe had her pregnant. She had a nerve to be crying saying that he told her to get an abortion. I didn't know what she expected me to do, but by that time I was so numb to the dumb cheating shit that Roscoe was doing in the streets. I wasn't hurt at all and told her that he was the person that she would need to talk to because it had nothing to do with me.

It's crazy because while I didn't give a fuck about Roscoe, the love of my life having a baby one me, Zoe, getting someone pregnant worried me to death. I felt myself on the verge of going crazy as the passing nurse confirmed that I was indeed crazy. I smoothed my hair down and said a silent prayer before I finally entered the room. Zoe was sleeping so peacefully, and I just wanted to smack all of the peace from his ass.

I stood over him unaware of what my next move would be when his eyes opened. As soon as he saw me his eyes got big as saucers as he reached out for me. I moved back and his smile turned into a frown.

"What's up Ash, why you all the way over there? Come give your man a hug." I only shook my head no and Zoe, stared as if he was trying to read me.

"Ash, you gone tell me what's wrong or what? First, I wake up and you're not here and now you acting funny style. What's wrong bae?"

Zoe sounded genuinely concerned, but I wasn't about to fall for his concerned act. "Pisces came to visit the other day," I said.

"And?"

"And, she had a lot to say about the two of you."

"Maannnn, I know you not tripping ov-"

"Wait, let me finish before you start making up lies. She told me that since you and I got together, the two of you haven't stopped fucking and guess what the hell else she said."

Zoe only looked at me with a face full of irritation like I was the one who was cheating and had a baby on the way.

"Don't get quiet now!"

"Well spit the shit out!" Zoe must've yelled a little too hard because he started to grunt while holding his side. I wanted to run to his aid, but I had a damn point to prove so I had to be tough.

"Zoe, she said that she was pregnant and its yours."

Zoe looked at me and no words were spoken and that all I needed to hear to know that Pisces wasn't lying.

"Oh my god," I said holding my face. I promised I wouldn't cry but the shit hurt like hell.

"Ash. Bae. Don't cry, we don't even know if it's mine. That bitch is a hoe." I didn't know what Zoe thought he was doing, but it wasn't reassuring me at all.

"Why did you lie Zoe? You told me that you weren't fucking with anyone else and that you had dropped them all when we got serious.

"Bae, you have to believe me. I did. If she is pregnant it's from when I was fucking with her before you."

"So, you telling me that since you and I were together, you haven't fucked her?" I asked seriously.

Zoe's head dropped in his hands. The nigga couldn't even face me.

"Zoe, you know what, I don't care if it's your baby or not because I'm done."

"What the fuck you mean you done?" he retorted.

"You heard me, go be with the bitch and your baby. I am done!"

I turned to walk away, and Zoe called my name loudly, but I knew that I couldn't turn around because I was liable to fall for his charm. I walked out of the room never looking back until I saw a doctor rushing toward me. When he ran right pass me and into Zoe's room, my heart jumped. I peeked back in the room and Zoe was shaking violently while doctors and nurses rushed to his aid. Before I could even ask what was going on just that quick, the door was closed.

MOCHA

It was the day of Zoe's funeral and even though I didn't know him that well, he was always cool when I saw him. I wobbled to the bathroom still wiping the sleep from my eyes when before I could even make it to the toilet, last night dinner came up. I quickly cleaned myself up and then got dressed in a black midi dress along with a forest green cardigan. After unraveling my bantu knots letting the soft curls fall along my back, I headed to Ashlyn's house and braced myself for what was to come. Ash was torn up over Zoe's death and she was barely able to get out of bed. I entered her once lavish home and clothing as thrown all over the place. The room reeked of liquor and darkness consumed the entire home.

Ashlyn was still in bed like I suspected buried under her comforter. I called her name softly and she didn't even move until I yanked the covers back. There lay her frail body as she snatched the cover back.

"Ashlyn, babe, it's time to get up and get ready for the funeral," I said softly.

"I'm not going,' she simply responded.

"Ashlyn come on! I now you are sad, but you will regret it if you don't come."

"Mo, you can talk all day but I'm not fucking going!" she screamed.

I bit my tongue because I know that she was sad, so I left her alone. I was just glad that Ross was staying with her mom for a few weeks. I found myself picking up Ashlyn's place as it looks like a world wind had hit it. Three was old food containers, clothing thrown all over the place and the garbage was stinking up the place. Zoe's funeral was in two hours and I had to somehow get Ashlyn out of the bed. While putting the dishes into the dishwasher, an idea popped in my head. If there was someone who could get her ass out of the bed it was LA. I really didn't want to call him because he probably wouldn't answer but I had to try.

The phone rang as I stood there with knots in my stomach. I didn't know why I was so nervous, but I just was.

"Yo," LA answered, and it sent trembles down my spine. LA had the deep baritone sounding like the damn Allstate man when he didn't look like that at all.

"Hey, Leandre. Its Mocha."

"I know who this is! What's up," he asked as if he was in a hurry or something. My nerves were now skyrocketing.

"Ummm, Ash isn't well and refusing to get out of bed today," I spit out.

"Okay, what do you want me to do Mo?"

"I don't know, but you guys were close, and you may be able to get through to her. She needs closure from this."

LA let out a sigh and there was a brief silence.

"I'm on my way," he said, hanging up before I could even say goodbye.

About twenty minutes later, LA scrolled in looking like a HQ model himself. I knew that he would hate if I complimented him, so I kept it to myself and admired from a distance. He wore a tailored black suit and Ferragamo loafers.

"Where is she?" he said when he finally laid eyes on me.

"Umm, she's in her bedroom." LA's eyes lingered on me like he wanted to say something but decided against it. Before he could walk away, I stopped him. "LA, me and Slim, were not..." before I could finish, he stopped me.

"Mo, this ain't about us right now," he said, and then walked away. I felt so damn dumb. Here I was being selfish when today was the day of his best friend's funeral.

I waited downstairs sitting on the couch for about forty-five minutes before I heard the cascading of feet down the stairs. Hand and hand came, LA and a now dressed Ashlyn. She wore shades and a somber look on her face. The two walked right past me and to LA's car. I knew damn well I wasn't riding with them, so I marched to my car and sped off a little disappointed. I had feelings for LA and he clearly didn't have any for me.

The funeral was packed like a selling party on a Saturday night as some people were even standing up. His friends and family shared sweet stories about him, and I felt like I knew him even more. LA sat holding his mother and Ash's hand while shades covered his face. He refused to cry, but deep down I knew that he was hurting. As everyone went up to view his body, I glanced back, and my eyes must've been playing tricks on me. In walked a very pregnant Pisces weeping like Zoe was the love of her life. Her loud cries made people look in her direction as she walked closer and closer to Zoe.

I turned in the direction of Ashlyn and anger was written all over her face. She stood up quickly headed to Pisces. I moved swiftly to intercept her because I didn't want Zoe's funeral tuning into a shit show. I grabbed my cousin before Ash could lay them paws on her and dragged her outside. The sky was gray, but the rain refused to drop.

"P, what are you doing here?" I asked when we were finally outside. I felt a sharp pain in my stomach that caused me to double over."

"Girl you okay?" P asked while rubbing my back.

"I'm okay," I lied. I didn't want her ass to try to avoid the question. "Why are you here?" I questioned again.

"What do you mean? I came here to show my respect."

"And what is this?" I asked, pointing to her stomach.

"What the hell do it look like? I'm pregnant and yes, its Zoe's baby."

"And how do you know P? You claimed that you were so in love with his damn best friend."

"Girl, I know what I been doing with my pussy and you don't have to worry, I don't want your man."

"Girl, well you need to go. You've paid your respects now leave because I can't stop Ashlyn form whooping your ass."

"Damn, is she your cousin, or am I?"

"P don't start with the family shit. Yeah, we cousins, but that does not mean that we are friends. You always got some sneaky shit with you and not to mention you're a damn liar."

"Ohhhhh, I get it. You're madder about LA then I thought."

"No, I'm not mad because there is not a LA thing. You were never with him, that is just something that you made up as usual. However, I am a little concerned though. Mentally, you not all there to make up such a story over a man. But I'm done, stay or go, I don't give a fuck." I walked back to the church leaving P, looking like she wanted to say more but dared not too. Before I could make it back into the church, this morning's breakfast came running out of my mouth right on the porch steps. My stomach had been bothering me all morning and I was kind glad that the shit finally came up.

Looking up the church doors were opened, and it was LA. I hurriedly got up and wiped my mouth. I tried zooming by him out of embarrassment, but he stopped me.

"Yo, what is going on with you?"

"What do you mean?" I asked, kinda thrown off by what he was asking.

"You know what I mean."

"I don't," I said, looking down at the ground. LA gave me the once over before shaking his head and walking back into the church, leaving me with a little bit of hope that he hadn't forgotten about me.

PEACHES

I sat in my car gawking at the way that LA looked at the skinny bitch Mocha. I thought that were over, but apparently, he was still into her. She looked at the ground like a fucking child as he towered over her was like was her protector. Each time she would look away, a slight smile formed on his face like he had found a damn treasure. The shit made me sick to my stomach, but I had something for both of their asses.

I drove off and called Sherman's ugly ass. He just didn't know that he was just a pawn in my grand scheme.

"Hey baby, I cooed into the phone."

"What's up?" he answered lowly.

"What's wrong baby?"

"Man, you know I'm still fucked up from what happened to my lil folks the other night."

I was so sick of hearing this nigga talk about his cousin Lou and two of his homeboys being gunned down. I mean, I knew that he was side but damn he needed to get over it. Them niggas was not coming back.

"Aww baby, you know I can make you feel better."

"Oh yeah," he said, perking up. "How so?"

"You just get ready for big mama later and you will see. But for now, I have some info that might interest you. Word around town is that one of your soldiers is playing both sides. Yahseem sister fuck with an NHG nigga and all of them went out to eat together a few weeks back. Need I say more."

"Word!" he said, as if I had just laid the biggest bomb on him. "Good looking out bae, I'ma definitely look into that. You think this shit got anything to do with Lou and them?"

"Could be bae, If Yahseem playing both sides, he could've given NHG Lou's math or whatever."

"Yeah man, you right," Sherman's dumb ass agreed. This nigga was like putty in my hands.

"You know I got you bae."

"Word, now get that ass over here so you can sit Lil' Peaches on my face."

To think all I had to do was throw some pussy at this goofy nigga and he would carry out my plans. My pussy got wet just thinking about the shit that was about to go down.

LA

I sat watching cartoons after my favorite girl Ross called and told me that her nana was being mean to her. Now she had me letting her paint my nails watching *Raven's house*.

"Baby, you not tired yet?" I complained. It was damn near ten at night and she looked to be wide awake.

"Nope," she answered, and then added some sparkle shit on my nails.

"Uncle La, where's Mocha? I heard mommy saying that you finally got it right this time, but I didn't k ow what she meant."

I chuckled at my niece's innocence and how she was snitching all at the same time. I perked up a little at the mention of Mocha's name and I wondered if she was with that nigga Slim, but for real that wasn't my situation.

"I don't know where she is Bug," I answered.

"I saw her a long time ago before uncle Zoe went away. She was really sick and said that she had a tummy ache and mommy gave her a soda."

My thoughts drifted to her and that little prance that she did when she walked. It was like she was floating on air with a little twitch in her hips, but her walk was a little different the last time that I saw her. Her legs were a little more gapped open and her motion was just a little slower. I then remembered how sick she was at the funeral and now Ross was telling me that she was also sick at least one time before that.

Now my mind was wondering, *was there anything going on with her. Was she sick? Like what the hell was going on with her.* I dropped my lil' folks off at my mama's house and then headed to Mocha's house, but not before going to CVS. I arrived at her house about twenty minutes later, hands all sweaty and shit thinking that she probably wasn't home; that was erased when I saw that all her lights were on and she was Blasting some Beyoncé or some shit.

I lifted the flower pot on her porch and found the obviously hidden key. Once, I was inside I smelled the scent of bleach and pine-sol floating through the air. This girl was cleaning and blasting this bullshit at 11:00pm at night, I know her neighbors were pissed, but it was a Friday. I made my way to the kitchen to see Mo sitting Indian style on the floor in the refrigerator. Random food items were sitting on the floor as she wiped the fridge out while singing her heart out.

"Because you lied, I only give you a hard time, cause I can't go on and pretend like I haven't tried to forgive this cu sim just to full of resentment."

I didn't get why she was singing her heart out to this shit and her singing was horrible by the way; I swooped her up on her feet. She opened her eyes and stopped doing what she thought was singing and pushed me off her.

"What are you doing here? How did you get into my house?" she yelled over the music before storming to her phone to stop it.

"Helloooo," she said, while waving her hands. What are you doing here?"

I couldn't help but stare at her in those tiny PINK shorts and cut off crop top. Her hair was in a messy bun all over her head, but she looked perfect to me. Her tiny frame went up and down as she huffed as if she was out of breath while looking at me like I was crazy.

"Calm yo' lil' ass down! I came to talk to you."

"What? Is something wrong with Ross or Ash?" A look of worry came over her face.

"Nah they good, but what if something was wrong with me?"

"That would be none of my business. Now why are you here again?"

"I'm here for this," I said, pulling three pregnancy tests from my pocket.

She looked at me weirdly, "What you think you pregnant or something?" she asked smartly.

"Nah, I think someone else in this room is so let's just get this over with Mo."

"What! Are you out of your mind? I'm not peeing on that stick for you. I would know if I was pregnant of not and why would you care anyway?"

"What the fuck you mean? If it's mine, I want to know. So, take your ass in the bathroom and let's get the shit over with."

She stomped upstairs like a bratty kid and I followed closely behind her watching that ass bounce up and down in her shorts. She looked back at me and frowned as If she could read my nasty thoughts.

"Once I take this damn test to show you that I'm not pregnant, you're getting out of my house."

"Yeah, yeah, shut up and pee."

"Um can I get some privacy please?" she barked.

"No," I answered dryly. She rolled her eyes and then snatched the test out of my hand. I stood there anxiously handled her business. When she was done with all three tests, she sat the them on the sink and we just looked. It was one of those two-minute janks and as the seconds went by it felt like a life time. Finally, tired of waiting, I grabbed the tests and two said yes and the other had two dark lines. Mo was really pregnant. I Looked back for her expression and I couldn't read her. I passed the tests to her and she let out a huge breath.

"Oh my god I'm pregnant," she said lowly.

I was happy, but my thoughts went back to the day that I saw he and slim in the mall. "Is it mines Mo?"

She whipped her head in my direction so quickly that I thought it would fall off.

"Get out!" she said, rising from the toilet and stomping down the stairs.

"Yo, hold up man!" I grabbed her arm. "Fuck you going off for? You don't think that I have the right to ask that question?" I asked seriously.

"Hell no! You were the one who left me! It wasn't the other way around. I haven't been with anyone since you, can you say the same?"

I couldn't say anything because she was right.

"Yeah, that's what I thought! Don't worry about it, we can get a test done if I even keep this shit!"

Now she was just talking crazy, "Yo, say some dumb shit like that again! if you ever think about killing something that belongs to me, you will go with it."

"LA you don't scare me. This is my decision and whatever I want to do will be up to me. Don't try to be all concerned now when you left me for nothing." I could tell that she was still hurting.

I messaged my temples because she was starting the crying shit and her tears always affected me. "Mo, it's not about us anymore. If we have a seed on the way. I don't want to fight with you" I pulled her into me, and she melted into my arms. Her tears didn't stop until she fell sleep in my arms before I slipped off into the night.

PISCES

I hit my stomach for the third time because this baby was kicking the shit of me, I was now five months and I couldn't wait to find out the sex of the baby. If it was a boy, he would be a Jr and if it was a girl, it would be named Zola.

"Pisces if you don't get your butt up off of that couch and go look for a job or something!" My mom shouted, interrupting my thoughts.

"I don't know who you expect to take care of that damn baby, the daddy is gone so there is only you left."

"Mama! Damn! Don't you see I'm trying to rest? You come in here bitching every damn day. Don't worry about me and my child, we good!"

"Well if you're so good, why are you twenty-six years old and living with me? Huh?"

I got up from the plastic covered sofa and it made a crunching sound as I lifted my wide load. "Mama, I'm not trying to hear that. Trust me, I will be out of your hair once I get on my feet."

She only stared at me as I brushed past her to my room. I was tired as shit of stalking Ashlyn on Instagram all night. She hadn't been up there much except when she posted throwback pictures of her and Zoe. I reeked with envy at a picture from before they even got together. It was a group photo, but Zoe's eyes were dead set on Ashlyn as she smiled widely at the camera.

Zoe never looked at me like that and I never looked at him like that either to be honest. My mind used to be so fixated on LA that Zoe was merely a fixture to me. LA was the one that I had wanted ever since the first night that I saw him at the NHG basketball tournament a few years back. See that's the part that the news anchors never talked about. Every time you turned on the news, you heard about another slain body or another victim to the streets, but they never showcased the community cookouts, back to school drives and clothing drives that NHG hosted for the kids every year. Yeah, they were heavy in the streets, but they had a lot more to them then the rep that they got.

I shifted in my bed before I finally got comfortable and fell asleep. When I woke up it was around five pm, so I decided to finally get up and get my day started. I rose form the bed still a little sleepy and stood to my feet only to crash back down. A sharp pain went through my stomach and straight up my back. "Ahh," I yelped in pain. The pain lasted for another five minutes before I tried standing again. My legs felt a little heavy, but I was able to make It to the bathroom without falling down. I sat on the toilet to relive myself and let out a deep breath. "Lil person in there, you better stop before I fuck you up," I said, talking to my stomach.

I wiped myself and stood to get in the shower when a rush of blood came flowing down my legs. It was like it was never ending as I closed my legs praying that it would somehow go back up. The next pain that was sent through my stomach caused me to go temporarily crippled as I fell to my knees and let out another yelp. I thought my mother would have heard me by now, but she never came. I lay on the bathroom floor with tears in my eyes hoping that what I thought was happening wasn't actually happening. I didn't want to lose my baby.

MOCHA

I hung up the phone with my mom after she yelled at me for changing my mind about coming back home for a while, but she didn't know that I was pregnant so I would wait to tell her after my appointment twirled around in the floor length mirror at the mint green baby doll dress that I was wearing, wondering if I was showing any. It had been two weeks since LA charged into my home and watched me take three pregnant tests and I was finally going to the doctors to confirm what we already knew. I tucked a lose stand of hair behind my ear and threw on my cross body before I was heading out of the house. To my surprise, there was a black Benz sitting in my drive way and out stepped LA. My face dropped.

"Fix your face and get in the car Mo, I know you didn't think that I was going to let you go to your first appointment alone," LA said, stepping around to the passenger side to open the door.

"That is exactly what I thought. You don't have to come you know?" I eyed him.

"Mo just cause we ain't together don't mean that I'm not going to do what I have to do. You got me confused with a busta' ass nigga. Now get in the car before we are late."

I hesitantly walked to the car and got in and within ten minutes we had arrived at the doctor's. We sat in the waiting area and waited to be called back. I kept catching LA staring at me.

"You're weird," I said, catching him for the third time.

He smirked, "Why I got to be weird? Why can't I just think that you're beautiful?"

I noticed the seriousness in his tone and decided to drop the conversation. On the car ride over LA made it clear that he wanted to do nothing but co-parent with me. For some reason he couldn't come to fully trust me after seeing me with Slim that day in the mall. But now he was staring at me all lovingly like I was the only one for him and it was confusing the hell out of me.

We were called back shortly after and my nerves stared to kick in as the doctor rubbed the cool Gel on my stomach. Instantly, we heard the heartbeat of our little one and LA grabbed my hand. I tried to fight back the tears, but my cancer ass could never miss an opportunity to cry.

The Appointment was short and sweet, and I learned that I was seven weeks pregnant which was right around the time when LA and I broke up. We drove home in silence, LA smiling like a fool as he bobbed his head to the music. He dropped me off home and as I was getting out of the car, he stopped me.

"Aye you want some food or something?" he asked.

"No, LA I have food in the house," I laughed.

"Oh, I thought you would want some pickles and peanut butter or some crazy shit like that."

"I'm not quite there yet, but thank you," I said.

"Aite call me if you need me," he said, and then drove off.

I cozied on the couch and wondered if I should tell anyone that I was pregnant. I knew that some people thought that it would be sorta jinxing myself since it was so early in my pregnancy. I wondered what my parents would say being that I wasn't married. My mother wasn't a saint herself, but she did value the sanctity of marriage. I decided to keep it to myself for now. I was really pregnant with a little pebble inside of me and though at first, I was a little nervous, now I couldn't wait to become a mommy.

ASHLYN

My baby was finally back home after she had been shipped from house to house while I got myself together. The pain of losing Zoe was still there, but I knew that I had a little girl that was watching me each day and it was unfair to her for me to be an unfit mother. Our move was paused indefinitely because I needed to be around my family at this time.

"Buuuugg! Wake up." I called out while snuggling beside her in her princess bed that reassembled a carriage. Ross stayed sleep and didn't even budge until I started tickling her stomach in which she started to move like ants were in her pants.

"Okay, okay mommy, I'm up!" she said, laughing like crazy.

"What do you want to do today Bug," I said, as I watched her attempt to brush her teeth independently.

"Umm let's go to the movies, and let's go see nana and Uncle La."

I shook my head at my five-year-old who was in a twenty-five-year old's body. I went in to hug her just needing some type of warmth. She stopped brushing her teeth and kissed my forehead getting toothpaste all over me.

"Mommy are you still sad because uncle Zoe went away?" she asked, her voice full of innocence.

"No baby, I'm not sad. I'm actually just happy to be your mommy," I said, pinching her cheek.

"You're so silly mommy, I am happy to be your Bug too," she turned around and then began to rinse her moth out. I wiped away my tears and made a note to perk the hell up so that my baby could enjoy her day.

Our first stop would be to the grocery store and then we could go wherever Ross wanted to go. I hadn't talked to LA since the day of Zoe's funeral and though he was there for me that day, I still didn't know how he felt towards me. We pulled up to Harris Teether and I noticed the frown on Ross's face. She hated the grocery store because she claimed that we always spent a hundred thousand hours there, her exact words.

"Bug, I promise to only be in here for thirty minutes. When we get in you can start your stop watch," she perked up then and began to undo her seat belt. Once we were inside, she played away on her tablet as I pinched fruits like my big mama taught me.

"Mommy, can I get fruity pebbles," Ross asked, finally looking up from her tablet.

"Sure Bug, but you have to make a deal with mommy. You have to eat all of your vegetables at dinner."

"Eww mommy even the broccoli. I hate broccoli."

"Whelp guess you don't want fruit pebbles, "I said, and then walked ahead of her.

"Okay, okay I will eat all of my vegetables," she said, while sulking. I smiled at her little sassy tail. We got Ross's cereal and then made our way to check out. Ross had reminded me that we only had seven minutes left in the store.

As we were walking, I got this weird vibe that someone was watching me and I turned to see a staring Pisces big as hell, stomach poking through her shirt.

"Who is that weird lady mommy?" Ross asked, taking a hold of my hand.

"Don't say weird Ross. That is not nice," I scolded her.

"Well don't you think that it is the "w" word that she is looking like that?" Ross asked.

I continued to check my things out, ignoring Ross but more focused on Pisces. The bitch looked bat shit crazy just staring at me rubbing her stomach. Usually, I would play into her antics, but today she looked like she was with the shits and I would not do anything in front of Ross.

Ross and I made it to the car and just as I expected, the crazy girl followed us out, but stayed at least five feet away from us. I sped off out of the parking lot, knowing that the bitch didn't have a car. The shit was spooky as hell, but I let it escape from my mind and enjoyed my day with Ross.

LA

The hype had died down a little about the killing of Lou, but I knew that the quiet wasn't necessarily a good thing. That just meant that some big shit would go down when people least expected it. I sat in the living room watching the news while my OG burned in the kitchen as usual.

"Awe man!" I heard her say from the kitchen and I jumped up thinking that something was wrong.

"What's wrong!" I asked.

"I don't have any sour cream for the mac and cheese," she complained, like she hadn't just scared the shit out of me.

"Fuck ma!" that's why you up in here hollering like you crazy."

"Boy, curse in here one more time and I'ma show you crazy," she tossed her small fist on my chest. "Now go to the store and get me some sour cream if you want dinner tonight," she handed me a ten-dollar bill and I looked at her crazy. "Ma quit playing," she knew I wasn't taking her damn money and she was passing me $10 like I was a hump or something. Don't even remember the last time I saw a damn ten.

"No, you stop playing and where is that nice chocolate girl that I met once? You know I dreamed of fish last night?" she took off her apron and sat down.

"Ma, you always dreaming of fish. You ain't happy with Ross?"

"Yes, I'm happy with my grandbaby, but that doesn't mean that you do not have some girl pregnant out here," she said matter fact.

"Ma, she not just any girl. Mocha is pregnant," she almost knocked me over jumping for joy when she heard that.

"Oh, I'm so happy son. That is a nice girl with a good head on her shoulders and she not too bad on the eyes."

"Dang ma! What about me? Am I going to contribute to the baby at all?" asked slightly offended.

"Oh boy hush up and gone and get that sour cream and make sure you get Daisy!" she yelled before disappearing back into the kitchen.

I got her damn sour cream and called Mo for the third time only to get her voice mail. The shit was lowkey irritating, but then again, she didn't have to stop what she was doing just to answer my calls. I pulled up to Ish's to grab me something to eat before dinner. Knowing my mama, a nigga wouldn't eat till damn near ten pm and it was on three. Raheem hooked me up with my usual and I couldn't wait to get back to the crib to smash. I licked my lips at the thought of it.

The chiming of a bell rang as I opened the it to leave, but I was stopped at the sound of laughter. It was a laugh that I had come to love and hate. I turned around and made my way back in and wandered through until I found the source of laughter. Mocha was standing there laughing with some mixed looking nigga and his hand was on her stomach. I marched over to them a smacked his hand away with so much force that he almost fell back.

"LA, what are you doing here?" Mocha asked, kind of caught off guard.

"Nah, what the fuck are you doing here and who is this nigga?"

"LA this is Mike. We used to work together," she snapped.

"Man, I don't care who he is. Fuck is he touching you for?" I didn't even care that I had just asked her wo the nigga was because I was fuming.

"Because it's my body. Now you need to lower you voice embarrassing me," she said starting to whisper like I cared about embarrassing her dingy ass.

"You embarrassing yourself, all up in here with niggas feeling up on you." Dude only stood there looking like he was about to pee his pants.

"Why you still here nigga?" I asked and then he scrammed barely making eye contact with Mocha. She stormed pass me and got into her car, but little did she know I was coming right behind her.

She made it to her house in no time and tried to shut the damn door on me, but she was no match for my strength. "Yo, you better stop playing with me," I said, once we were finally in.

"No one asked you to come here so get out!"

"Man, I'm not going nowhere."

"I don't know what the fuck you want from me. We are not together so you have no right to question me about anything that I do!" she jerked her neck.

"I have all the rights when you carrying my seed."

"Boy please. You act like you still like me or something when you've made it very clear that you only want to co-parent."

Mocha had it all wrong, I didn't just like her, I love her smart ass. I had tried to move past her, but once she let me know that she was pregnant it was a lost cause. No matter how much I played it off or how many bitches I fucked to replace her, it would never happen, and her carrying my child only intensified it.

"So why do you have a problem with other people touching me? What is it to you?" she went on and on whining and shit.

"Mo, you want to know why I don't like other niggas touching you? Cause I want to touch your black ass. I want to lay with you every night. I want to raise this child with you. I just want you Mo!"

She stood there silently, void of any emotion and I felt crazy. "You are so up and down that it drives me insane. You come in here spilling all of this on me and it too much. How do I know you won't just up and stop talking to me like you did last time? How do I know you're really in this with me for real?"

"Mo, you won't know until you let me show you and I'm willing to work until we get it right," I said sincerely.

"Get out Lance. Right now, I'm pregnant and hormonal and I don't want to see you right now. Just go!" I looked at her for a moment before I left in defeat.

After getting cursed out by my mama for never bring the damn sour cream, I just wanted to go home to crash and that is exactly what I did. As soon as my head hit the pillow I was out like a light. I woke up and the clock read 3:08 am and went to take a leak when I heard soft knocks at the front door. The knocks then suddenly stopped. I raced down the stairs and opened the door to see Mocha running to her car while trying to shield herself from the light drizzle.

"Mo!" I called out to her.

She turned around and for a moment we only stared until I walked out to her. Wearing nothing but boxers I did not care, but I knew I had to get my girl back. She looked down at her feet and I lifted her chin.

"You really want to do this?" she asked softly.

"Mo, I've loved you from the from, well second day that I saw you." We both laughed. "Of course, I want to do this and if we get it wrong, we can try again and keep trying. I'm here." Immediately Mocha's shoulders dropped as if whatever she was carrying had disappeared. I scooped her up in my arms and carried her inside so that she could dry off. When I was toweling her down, she looked at me intensely before I took her into my mouth.

"Let's get in the shower bab- I mean Lance," she knew I hated that baby shit. We got into the shower and the water sprouted out from the four walls and I rested my hands on two side of the wall. Mocha looked at me hungrily and it was then that I noticed the tiny pudge in her stomach. It could've just been me but knowing that something that I created was growing inside of her made my dick hard. I dropped down to my knees and planted kissed on her tiny belly. Her clean waxed pussy was looking dead at me as I lifted her onto my shoulders and was finally met with her juicy pussy. I could tell that she had missed my tongue skills as she shook in pleasure as I circled my all around her slit.

"Ahhh! I'm about to come baby!" she yelled out.

I smacked her ass "What did I tell you about calling me that shit!"

"Ouuhh, ba- I'm sorry daddy," she was trying to run from me now as I yanked her closer in my face.

I went deeper and deeper with my tongue and just like she chanted she came on my tongue immediately. I let her down from my shoulders and stopped at my waste. Her breath tickled the back of my neck when I entered her. Pumping in and out of her slowly, her body jerked a little. "Am I hurting you?" I asked, fearing I was touching the baby or some shit.

"Umm umm," she moaned, winding her hips forward. I increased the speed of my strokes while Mo planted her teeth into me. My man fit her like a glove and If I could, I would stay there forever. I pumped in and out of her forcefully as my dicked touched every part of her walls.

"Oh, yessssss Laaa!" Mo screamed and we both came simultaneously. We stayed still for a moment, my dick still inside of her while she planted soft kisses on my chest. Slowly, she climbed off of me and came face to face with my dick before she took it in pretty ass mouth. Her pretty lips look so good wrapped around my tool that I almost came instantly. Mocha jerked her head back and forth as my dick hit the back of her throat.

"Ahhh shit bae," I moaned as she gobbled my balls into her mouth. I felt myself on the verge of busting and pushed her head back. "Let me swallow it," she demanded and caught each drip of my cum making sure to suck me dry.

"Damn girl!" I said smacking her fat ass "That pregnant pussy ain't no joke," I joked. We stayed in the shower for another twenty minutes as I washed our bodies clean before we both crashed into the night, her tucked away in my arms.

PEACHES

I walked into the dark and dampened basement to see a crazed looking Sherman sitting at a rounded wooden table with an AKA 47 on his lap, facing two lines of coke. The floor creaked as I walked, and I felt beads of rain hit me from the leaky ceiling. There was a bulletin board on the wall and attached to it were pictures of LA, Ashlyn, Zoe, Mocha, and a few other NHG members. Zoe had a big red X across his face and each picture was connected buy a string.

This shit was something out of the criminal minds or something. Sherman's eyes were blood shot red as he looked like he had been crying. He held a Hennessy bottle in his hand as his glossy eyes finally connected with mine. For the first time of messing around with him, I genuinely felt a little creeped out his insane stare.

"Why you are standing over there?" his words slurred. "C'meeeerre."

I walked over to him slowly and he yanked me closer to him.

"When you gone give me some of this pussy girl?"

"Bae, you're really drunk right now. Maybe you should go and sleep it off," I suggested.

"I'm good and ready to fuck so drop them drawers!" he demanded.

I guess the time had finally come because for weeks I had promised him some pussy, but I somehow always talked him out of it. Tonight, would go down very differently as he gazed at me with his lust filled eyes.

I slowly removed my top and then started to unzip my pants when Sherman ripped my hands away and yanked my pants to my ankles.

"Don't got time to be playing with you," he mumbled. He then grabbed my hand and led me to an old raggedy couch and pushed me back. He then took out his swollen dick, which was the size of a fucking hotdog, the Gwaltney kind. He stroked it ferociously before he leaned down and instructed me to open my mouth. I did as I was told, and he spit a big gush of spit in my mouth. Usually I was into kinky shit like that, but not coming from Sherman, but I knew that I was on a mission. In any other situation this nigga's nuts would've been cut off or something.

Next, he hungrily kissed me while fondling my breast. I pretended like I loved it so we could hurry and get the shit over with. He roughly stuck his little pecker in me and pumped away like nobody's business. I moaned a little which super boosted his ego. He started calling out shit like, "What is my name?" and "Tell me this my pussy!" I played his little game before he pulled out and came on my stomach. He left me laying there while his stomped his fat ass up the stairs. He returned about five minutes later with a warm rag for me to clean myself up.

He then went back over to where he was siting earlier and snorted the two lines of coke. This nigga then busted out in a fit of cough like he was going crazy. I hurriedly got up and made sure that he was okay and then made a quick exit. I couldn't wait for our plan to finally escalate and then I would definitely finish his ass.

LA

I woke up in a cold sweat from the dumbest dream that I had had. In the dream I was running and running and when I reached the end of a long ass hallway there standing was Mocha, wearing all white. Her skin glowed and she looked as if she was floating on air. Once I got to her, she would disappear, and Peaches would appear. The shit was crazy as hell and I kept having the same reoccurring dream for the past few days. I didn't know if this was god's way of telling me that I needed to come clean to Mo about peaches or what, but the shit was getting on my nerves.

I turned over to face Mo and her side of the bed was empty. I rubbed the space where she was laying, and it was still warm letting me know that she hadn't been gone for too long. I made up my mind that I would tell her the truth about Peaches and I tonight. I stared at the ceiling waiting for her to come back but when ten minutes passed, I got a little worried. I got up and checked the bathroom, but she wasn't there. Lately she was pissing like twenty times a day, so I was surprised when I didn't see her there.

I then went to the kitchen, her second favorite place, but she wasn't there either. Now I was a little irritated. She knew better than to leave out this damn late without me carrying my precious cargo. I raced up the stairs to slip on some sweats when I heard something coming from the guest bathroom down the hall. *I know she was not doing this shit again!* The door was cracked open and creeped toward it. Mocha was crouched down over the toilet and at first, I thought that she had eaten something and had an upset stomach, but I was soon disturbed when there was no food coming out, Just a watery yellow colored substance. She wasn't throwing up anything but water. I knew that she had an eating disorder in the past, but I did not know that It was still a problem for her. The first time that I had caught her throwing up, I left the shit alone because she said she could handle it but now shit was getting out of hand

"Yo, what the fuck are you doing!" I asked, yanking her up. Her eyes were glossy, and residue was all over her face. "And don't lie to me Mocha. Why the fuck you in here throwing up?" I didn't understand the shit.

"It's not what you think baby. I just had something bad to eat."

"What the fuck you eat then because I checked the trash and the fridge for leftovers," I lied.

"Bae, I promise, I just got a little sick," she whined, but I didn't believe her. It was just like an addict who needed a hit.

"Stop fucking lying!" I yelled forcing her to look at the toilet. "There ain't no fucking food in there. The fuck was you trying to throw up? This is not even about you anymore; I keep telling you that shit. You are carrying a life inside of you and you on some dumb shit!" I had to walk away before I did something that I would regret. I grabbed my keys and stormed out of the house with one destination in sight.

After twenty minutes of driving I ended up banging on Ashlyn's door. She peeked her head out of her blinds and finally opened the door.

"LA are you crazy? Why are you banging on my door like that?" she tried whispering. I looked at her through my blood shot red eyes and she moved out of the way and let me in.

"Sis, she pregnant," I finally said, sitting on her leather black sectional.

"What? Mocha is pregnant?" she shouted excitedly. "That is great news. You're not happy?"

"Man, I'm beyond happy, but she fucking herself up."

"What do you mean by that LA? Tell me what is going on."

Silence

"You know. we are working on us and shit, but tonight I caught her in the bathroom throwing up."

"Well LA, you know that in common in pregnancies, right?"

"Man, it ain't what you think. Mocha dealt with an eating disorder when she was younger, and I think she starting that shit again. We talked about the shit before, but it was brief."

Ashlyn gasped and came over and rested her hand on my back. "So what? What you gone do? Run or something? I know you mad, but you love that girl and she needs you. Having an eating disorder is not a choice for her. She's sick and going through something and she needs you to be there for her. You remember when Roscoe died and how bad off, I was, and you were there for me. You never gave up on me or your niece and cursed my ass off if you needed too. Mocha needs that same support."

I took in what Ashlyn was saying, but I was mad as hell right now. She was endangering our damn baby and I couldn't look past that. The next thing I knew Ashlyn walked away and reemerged with pillows and blankets. "Stay here tonight and sleep it off. Tomorrow you will wake up with a clear mind and then the two of you can talk about it."

Ash hugged me goodnight and then left me alone with my thoughts. I sat on the couch staring aimlessly at the wall, sleep nowhere near my mind. After contemplating with my thoughts, I made my way back home with Mocha. When I walked in, she was still up siting on the couch with tear tracks on her face.

"What you doing up?" I sat sitting beside her.

"Couldn't sleep," she answered with a shrug of her shoulders.

"You want to talk about it?" I could not believe how coolly I was acting now, but spazzing out wouldn't make shit get any better.

"If you want to," she said lowly.

"So, what is going on with you?" I pulled her close so that she could face me.

"Well," she started and tucked her hair behind her ear. "The pregnancy has made me happy overall, but with you and I getting back together and finding out about the baby made me kind of anxious. I'm not blaming you or the baby, but I just need to maybe start back seeing my therapist. I just get so wound up at times and that is when the purging and throwing up begins."

"So why you ain't tell me how you been feeling bae? I can't help you if I don't know what's going on with you."

"I know. But I thought I could handle it, but you see how that turned out." We both sat there with our thoughts, holding hands on some goofy shit. Mocha leaned over and rested her head on my lap "I'ma get better babe, I promise, if not for me for my baby.

MOCHA

I scanned the racks of baby clothes for my little Punkin' for things that looked more unisex, since I didn't know the sex yet. I had just come from a therapy session and now I needed to do something that I enjoyed and that was shopping. I had seven little cute outfits in my cart already and I had only scanned one rack. Shopping was definitely my weakness and if LA found out he would snap my neck. Punkin's closet was already filled to capacity. LA could not talk though because he splurged on the baby as well. He had already started a college fund for him or her. Now what if Punkin wanted to join the circus or something, He would not need college for that.

I scanned my last rack before I headed to check out. My phone rang and it was my aunt Pat, Pisces's mom. I hadn't spoken to her in months, so this was odd. "Hey aunt," I answered.

"Hey baby, how are you?" she greeted me sounding like the actress Loretta Devine.

"I'm great aunty, what going on? Is everything okay?"

"Well, that why I'm calling you. It's that crazy tail Pisces. You know she's pregnant, but lately she's been a little odd. She stays on that girl Ashlyn's Instagram page all day and she doesn't even go to her doctor's appointments. I noticed a change in her a few weeks ago, but I don't know what it is," she sounded concerned.

"Really? I haven't spoken to her since the funeral, I hope she's okay though."

"Well, that is why I called you. I want you to talk to her. You have always had a positive effect on her and maybe she will talk to you." I kissed my lips at her response. Lord knows that I did not want to talk to her, but I could never say no to aunt Pat who let me spend every summer at her house.

"Okay, auntie I will give her a call. Love you and talk to you soon." I ended the call and put the thoughts of P on the back burner because I was meeting Ashlyn for lunch. It seemed like I hadn't seen her in ages, and we needed to catch up. She didn't even know that I was pregnant. I pulled up to a little quaint sandwich shop that Ashlyn picked. When I walked in, she was seated at a table with her face so far in the menu that she didn't even notice my presence.

"Hey girl hey!" I started. Ash finally looked up and stood to hug me.

"Hey Mommy!" she said excitedly. I looked at her with the side eye because how did she know that I was pregnant.

"Oops, I wasn't supposed to say anything was, but yo baby daddy slipped up and told me. Don't be mad. He's so happy!" she bounced up and down.

"He talks to damn much with his worrisome self. I swear he calls me a million times a day," I said sitting down in the booth. "Well now that you know my news. How have you and Ross been doing?"

"Girl I'm making it. I've been pretty good lately, but out of the blue, I will think about Zoe's crazy ass. I'm seeing a therapist though so I'm getting through it."

"Girl me too, I wasn't feeling like myself lately and somethings started happening, so I hit my therapist up as well.

"Well Amen to therapy," she said and we both laughed. Ash and I chatted and ate and talked about everything under the sun for hours.

"Girl, and did I tell you I saw your cousin a few weeks back. She looked crazy as hell and scared my baby," Ashlyn said with this stank look on her face. She and Pisces couldn't stand one another.

"That's funny because I just spoke to her mother and she said the same thing. I wonder what the hell is going on with her. I think I might drop by her house later."

"Yeah girl, go see your crazy tail cousin and tell her to leave me alone," Ash said, while laughing, but really serious.

Two hours later, I was in front of Aunt Pat's house preparing myself to go in. I really didn't want to see or talk to P, but I was somewhat alarmed from Ashlyn's and her mom's stories. I wobbled myself up to the door. I was getting bigger and bigger by the day with a little bump poking underneath my dress. I knocked softly on the door, but after not getting an answerer I started to bam when I heard footsteps approaching the door.

"Who the fuck is it?" P's voice boomed.

"It's Mocha!" I answered, trying to match her authority.

There was silence before the door was swung opened. "Hmm, fancy seeing you here. How can I help you?" she asked in a snappy tone.

"Girl let me into this house," I said never minding her snarky tone.

She looked me up and down before finally moving aside and letting me in. I sat down on the couch and she was still looking at me with this weird look in her eyes.

"How are you P? I came over here to check on you, being that I haven't seen you in a while."

"Well that's funny. I thought you were over there living your best life with lil' LA." Now he was lil' LA because she could hop on his lil' dick.

"Wellll, I am," I said sarcastically, "but, I didn't come here to go back and forth with you. What is going on with you? How is the baby?" My eyes dropped down to her stomach as she was a little bigger than the last time that I had saw her. Soon, she would be having the baby in a month or two.

"We're just fine!" she emphasized.

"Well why haven't you been going to the doctor? Aunty called me."

"Girl she needs to mind her damn business. I go to the doctor every month like I'm supposed to. She's so busy working that she doesn't know what be going on!" P snapped.

"Well I know that we haven't talking in a while, but I'm here if you need me. No one should have to go through a pregnancy alone," I said, inadvertently rubbing my stomach. P eyed me suspiciously.

"Oooh, so that is why you really came over here huh?" she let out a loud laugh. You came over here to gloat about you being knocked up by LA! You came to remind me that my baby daddy is gone and yours is still here!"

"P, you can't be serious. I would never do that or even think that way. Your mom and I are just genuinely concerned about you."

"Well you can take your fake concern out of here bitch. She walked up to me and grabbed my arm.

"Girl get off me!" I screamed, but P was bigger than me and her grip was strong. "Bitch get out!"

I finally yanked away from her. "Bitch you are miserable. I hope you get yourself together before that baby comes."

"Bitch don't ever speak on mine." She hopped in my face and chest bumped me.

I had to leave before me and this girl started fighting and something happened to my baby. I walked to my car all the while, P spit venom at me. I planned to never see her ass again and my prayers would be with her child having to deal with a total nutcase.

PEACHES

I called up my fake homegirl Mocha and told her that I missed her and that we should hang out. The bitch didn't hesitate and said that she would love to go out. Mocha was so damn dumb, and it was obvious that her man was still hiding shit from her. Just thinking about LA made me think of the time when I used to feast on that python that he had in his pants. LA used to fill me up like no other even when he wasn't inside of me. It was just something about his vibe that put bitches like me under his spells. I couldn't understand how he just thought that I would give up his good dick having ass that easily.

How could a woman not fight for LA? He was just that damn good and his looks and pockets matched his cocky demeanor. He wasn't your average street dude that hung on the corner hollering at bitches all day. You hardly caught him doing anything that didn't concern his funds and the only nigga he really hung with was Zoe. He was a low-key gangster and that is what made me fall for him in the first place. His mother should've named him God.

I almost jumped for Joy when Mocha's green ass gave me the address to LA's house to come and pick her up. I wondered if the bitch had moved in yet. Out of the three years that I had been fucking with LA I had never gone to his house. We usually went to hotels or a little spot that belonged to NHG. Roscoe, LA's brother had got this nice little town house as a place for NHG members to come to after doing a bid or something. If you got put out by your bitch or simply didn't have anywhere to go, you went to that house.

I quickly texted the address to Sherman and he sent me back so many gun emojis. The shit made me we that Mocha would finally be out of the damn way. Once, something happened to mocha, I would drop a little bomb in LA's ear that I heard that it was Sherman who made the hit. LA would get at him and his people and then he and I would live happily ever together after once I licked his wounds from him missing Mocha.

I called Mocha when Sherman let me know that he was minutes away from LA's house. I wanted to hear this bitch die. "Hey girl," I answered the phone. "I'm about five minutes away."

"Okay boo, I'm putting on my shoes now," she replied.

"Girl you could hurry up if that big ass stomach wasn't in the way."

I heard LA's voice and an electric shock went down my spine This man made me feel warm all over, but I didn't even know his ass was home. He wasn't supposed to be home. This could mess up my entire plan. If Sherman saw LA slipping, he would surly kill him and that is not what I wanted.

"I'm coming out now girl," Mocha said, and then hung up the phone. I crept down their street and saw Mocha and LA coming out of the house, a big ass house. It was stone grey and easily looked like it had four or more bedrooms. LA and this bitch were living large while I only was the inside of his pants most times. His hand held her lower back while the other hand rubbed her belly. I looked a bit more closely and I almost fell out. *This bitch is pregnant!* I beat the stirring wheel with my fist and was so upset that I didn't even see the unmarked car driving by. Suddenly, Bullets rang throughout the quaint neighborhood and I ducked for dear life. The bullets seemed like that were never ending, but when I looked up, I saw LA shooting back while shielding Mocha. The unmarked car then screeched off while LA was still bussin'. The next thing I saw almost made me get out of my car and do the heel toe.

LA was carrying Mocha's limp body and a single tear dropped from his eye. He was so calm and handled her so lovingly, but I couldn't stay to watch the show because I didn't want to get caught. I drove off with a smile on my face that my plan was almost done, and I was closer to getting my man back.

LA

I sat in the hospital waiting room a fucking mess at the shit that had just happened. Niggas rolled up to my crib and shot my girl. I had managed to get hit once in the foot, but it was like the niggas wasn't even trying to hit me. They were surly aiming for my girl. It's like they knew when we would be coming out of the house like the shit was planned or something. My mind was everywhere when the nurse came to let me know that Mo was all patched up and would be fine but would need plenty rest and tending to.

Mocha had been shot three times, once in the shoulder and twice in the leg. Thank god her and the baby would be fine. She did have to go through surgery to get the bullet surgically removed from her arm and leg. I walked in and she was awake talking to her parent on the phone. I bet that they were on their first flight here and I would have to deal with her bitch ass brother who was now staying with them.

Mocha didn't even acknowledge my presence as she ended her phone call and just stared at the ceiling. "Baby how are you doing?" I said kissing her forehead.

"What happened today Lance?" she answered dryly.

"Man, I don't even know but trust niggas will be handled." I walked angry as hell pacing the floor.

"When are you going to learn that this hit never ends? You take one of theirs, they take one of yours and the shit just keeps going," she clapped her hands as she spoke.

"Well, it is what it is. They not gone touch mines and just think that shit is sweet."

Mocha shook her head and let out a chortle. "Okay, well this is going to end now."

I looked at her confused at what she was talking about. She tried sitting up, but her shoulder prevented her. She let out a gasp and I ran to her side.

"Nope, don't do that! Do not touch me!" she yelled.

"Yo, what the fuck is your problem? I didn't do shit to you," I asked.

"What is my problem? This is my problem!" she pointed to her bandaged leg. "You are my problem! I'm in damn hospital bed because of some childish ass beef that you have in the streets. You are living for a gang that doesn't have shit to give you but death. I put up with shenanigans when it was just me to think about, but now I have a baby to think about and you will not endanger either of us!"

"Mo, you know that I would not hurt you or my baby, but you just want me to sit back and watch people attack my family!"

"Yep, I do. End this shit," she went on.

"Baby, I'm already in too deep!" I pleaded.

"Don't call me baby Lance and if you can't end it you will not be a part of me or my child's life."

My ears were burning, and my temples were throbbing a thousand miles per hour. "Mocha, who the fuck do you think you are to say some shit like that to me, huh?" I beat my chest.

"Lance, do you see what happened today! I was simply walking and got shot. What if I was holding your baby? How would that have ended?

"Mo," he pleaded. "I will move ya'll if need be. You will be safe. I won't let nothing like this ever happen again.

Mocha only sighed and covered her face before crying. "Damn! Today was supposed to be a simple day of me and Peaches going to dinner and now look at me," she sobbed.

My ears perked up at the mention of Peaches' name. I didn't even know that they were back hanging around.

"You said that you were supposed to go with Peach?" I asked clenching my fists.

She looked at me, "Why do you care?"

I know that it could've been a long shot but was Peaches this jealous that she would set this shit up. If she was supposed to had been picking Mo up, why didn't the bitch ever show up! My thought ran rapidly, as I pieced together everything in my head. Mo was just looking at me trying to figure me out and I knew that I couldn't keep up this secrecy about Peaches. I had to tell her. "Mo, I really don't know how to say this, but just know that I never planned on hurting you or lying to you."

Mo saw right through me like no woman had before and she braced herself for the bad news. She wiped her tears and nodded her head signaling for me to go on. "I know Peaches. Well I knew her before you even came into the picture. Peaches and I used to fuck around," I spat out.

Mocha squinted her eyes and mirrored in on me. "Are you telling me that while I was befriending this chick, you two were fucking around?" she asked calmly.

"No Mo, I swear. I stopped fucking her when you and I met."

"Bullshit, I don't believe you. If you and her were so called over, why did it take you until now to tell me? Do you know how stupid you had me looking, everyone knew but me!"

I could not even respond because she was right, and I couldn't keep trying to make excuses for myself. I grabbed her hand hoping that we still had that connection when she snatched it away from me.

"Don't touch me! Don't ever touch me again! I've dealt with you breaking up with me, ignoring me and now your old bitch basically stalking me. I am done. I can't keep you from you child, but you and I are done," she had a look in her eyes that told me that she was tired.

"Mo don't do this. I can make it right.'

"Make it right for yourself and this game alone. It's dangerous and you will not win!" With that Mocha turned her back from me signaling the end of us. "Bye Lance."

YAHSEEM

I sat in a space that resembled somewhat of an abandoned factory. A gloomy light elevated the room making it hard for me to see out of my one good eye. My other eye was swollen shut and numerous bruises were pictured on my race. My clothing was disheveled and almost ripped to shreds as I sat tied to a chair. The damp factory was ice cold as the mice payed at my feet. I was in a fucked p situation because I didn't know where I was or who had brought me here.

I had got caught slipping in Philly. I had moved out of my sister's crib and moved back to VA with my family. The only reason that I was even in Philly was because I had to take this jawn to get an abortion. I made sure I came up here with her ass cause I wasn't putting a dime n her hand so that she could skirt off with my money and by an outfit.

I handled my business with her and then decided to hit up a bar and drunk one drink too many. I came staggering out of the bar and shit and then some nigga put a bag over my head and put me in a truck. Once they let me out, they beat my ass with the bag still over my head and now I'm here.

I heard footsteps approaching me in addition to a the strong scent of African Musk. That distinct smell was only accompanied by one person and now I knew exactly who sent out the order on me. The bag was taken off my head and I was face to face with King Louie, Lou's dad. He sat in front of me looking like slick rick or some with a Kango hat and gold all through his mouth. The old man had aged well partly due to the face that he was sitting on millions.

"Young man, I'm sorry that you were roughed up a bit, but I hope that my ears have deceived me. Word is, you are in bed with the enemy these days."

"King Louie, I don't know what you have heard and no disrespect but get this fucking rope off of me right now!" Lou chuckled along with his henchmen that were present as well.

"I could do that for you, but I'm not. I have a few questions for you and if you answer right, I won't let these mice feast on your ass for dinner tonight. How about that?"

I began to shake hoping that I could free myself of the, but it didn't work. I only ended up face first on the floor.

"Now Yahseem, if you are done with the child's play. Tell me how you know LA personally?"

"Man, I don't know that nigga like that. My sister fuck with him, but that don't have shit to do with me!" I yelled.

"Okay, and is it true that he was in your presence, matter of fact, face to face with you and you did nothing?"

"My fucking whole family was there, and we were in the public. How stupid of me would that have been to snake the nigga with thirty eye witnesses? I just got out from doing a bid and I'm not going back!" I said with some authority in my voice. I knew that king Louie was the big man around town, but I wasn't about to go out like no Pussy.

"So, tell me Yahseem? How important is your life that you spared his? Huh?"

"If I have to die for something that I believe in then I will, but I'm not harming innocent people all at the expense of one. I love my fucking life and I will surely meet all of you grimy motherfuckas on the other side."

King Louie held his hand up to silence me, "Say less," he then got up and walked away before one of his henchman opened a chest that he had been holding. Once he opened it, a million little rats roamed all over the room before they smelled my scent. One by one they started to cover my body. I shook myself to keep them off of me, but I was not match for the little furry creatures.

"I will see you in hell Louie!" I yelled at his back, but he only kept going forward.

LA

"I want to know everything that the streets know. I don't care how much blood shed there is. This shit gone be handled," I said to the two eager young bulls standing in front of me. War and Chaotic were their names and even though they were brothers, same mom and dad they couldn't have been more different. War was more other the quiet intellect. He researched every different type of way to kill a person without getting caught. War had even graduated from college with a degree in psychology, so he was more than aware at how the mind of a killer works. War was quiet when he needed to be but raised hell one moment and had his head in a book the next.

Now Chaotic on the other hand raised straight havoc since the day that he had come out of the wound. He was known as a bully in the streets and had an act first think later mind set which sometimes got him in trouble. While war was light with hazel eyes. Chaotic was black as tar with eyes as dark as the pits of hell. War and Chaotic both balanced one another out where as War used logic and Chaotic used instincts.

The two hungry cats assured me that they wouldn't come up empty and whoever had to fill it in order for us to get answers would. I was tired of killing the people who didn't matter just to send a message. This time I wanted whoever had pulled that trigger and shot Mo, head's on a platter and I would rest until it was done. I had murder on my mind, and I wouldn't switch the tune.

PEACHES

Shit definitely didn't go down the way that I had expected it. The city was on fire about that sit and LA had his boys knocking down everything that was moving. I figured that LA might come for me, so I had to get the hell out of dodge. I packed up a few things and headed to my aunt's house which was about an hour away. I couldn't believe that Sherman or whoever made the hit didn't kill Mocha. The bitch had only been shot three times according to the streets.

I made it to my aunt's house before night fall and I was tired as hell. I just wanted to get some grub, shower and then lay it flat. I entered the dimly lit house and aunt Liz was sitting in an old lazy boy chair in an old house coat. "Hey aunty," I greeted her. She nodded and went right back to watching the Wheel of Fortune show. I put my bags in the spare bedroom and then headed straight to the kitchen. Aunt Liz was always cooking so I knew that I could find some leftovers or something. I snooped in the fridge and found left over smoothed porch chop, corn and mashed potatoes. My stomach was now doing black flips. I closed the fridge, turned around and nearly dropped the corn. A stocky figure appeared in the door frame. The only light that was on in the kitchen was the oven light which really didn't help me at all.

"Hello Patricia," the voice said, and my legs instantly let out beneath me. "Have a seat," he finally came into the kitchen and pulled the seat out for me. Big C still looked the same and with his hard-black skin and teddy bear build. Big C had only did seven years out of his fifteen and I wondered why.

"Looking good P, what's it been, four or five years since I last seen you. You looking damn good," he said flicking a toothpick in and out of his mouth.

In the beginning of his bid, I was there going to see him two times a week, sending him canteen, holiday packages and some more, until I got tired of a jail house relationship and needed some dick.

"I never knew that my wife would dessert me like that,' he eyed me and then softly grabbed a hold of my hand.

"Waa, waa, well, a lot was going on at the time," I had almost forgot that my young dumb and in love ass had married this nigga the first year that he got locked up.

"No need to trip on your words baby. Daddy's home now." Big C had a sinister look in his eyes, and I knew that I wouldn't be returning to Philly anytime soon.

MOCHA

"So, I was asked on a date and its feels so funny. Of course, I said no. I am not dating no time soon. I've lost two men in a matter of my short lifetime," Ashlyn said.

"Girl, Let's not talk about losing men," I said as I limped over to the couch. I had been out of the hospital for three days and Ashlyn had been making sure that I was good, per LA's request. Him and I hadn't talked but he made sure that I was moved to a new location because he claimed that my old spot would be too hot. Only and Ash knew the new location. I missed him but every time I thought of him my thought went to that damn Peaches. This both had only befriended me to get close to LA. I wanted to ring her neck and I had even paid her a visit, but her apartment was empty. She better had hope that I didn't catch her in traffic after having my baby because homegirl and I had a lot to discuss.

"For real, it's like the stars have not aligned for me to be happy," she said sadly

"Girl you will be happy, you've taken enough losses and I think you should take these guys up on their date offers."

"Girl I would never. Zoe hasn't even been in the ground for six months. It just feels too soon, how would people look at me?"

"Why do you even care? Life is too short to not be happy. that's why I had to end that shit with LA. It was just too much, and he blatantly lied to me."

"Girl don't carry my brother like that. It was foul that he didn't tell you about Peaches, but Lance is a good man. He changed up everything for you."

"Okay, and I'm not giving him props on things that he supposed to do. I have bullet holes in me right now because of love. I loved and still do love someone who I shouldn't be with."

"Well, who says you shouldn't? I agree with walking away but don't give up on him. After all, ya'll will always be connected because of that big head little boy that you are carrying," she beamed as if she knew what she was talking about.

I snapped my neck so fast, "Oh my god Ash, please stop saying hat. I want a girl so badly and you and LA are going to jinx me."

"Yep, Nany boy gone come out looking just like LA and Sco. The mutherfuckers were twins."

I laughed and my thoughts went to LA. "I do miss him sometimes, I mean it's only been a few days, but we went from talking all damn day calling each other twenty times daily to now nothing nada. He sneaks in hear when he knows I'm at the hospital and fills the refrigerator and drop baby shit off, but that's it."

"Well, I know ya'll will get it together soon," she had so much hope in her eyes.

"Well anyway, who is this person that asked you on a date?"

"Girl I took his number. Let me see." Ash scrolled to her iPhone before saying, "Slim."

"Slim? Light skin, short cut?" I asked.

"Yep that's his ass. You know him?"

"Yeah, that's the dude LA caught me in the mall with. He was cool, but I think he had a girlfriend."

"Girl, he told me that he had just broke up with a girl that he had been with for years and he was looking to just vibe with someone. Nothing too serious."

"Bitch, I say go for it. Buuuuuut, there is one thing. He's NBK."

Ash sighed, "Girl, I'm so tired of this gang shit. All the niggas either

NBK or NHG. Can't fuck with nobody," she huffed. I laughed at her true her statement was.

Two hours later I was in bed watching Re-runs of the hit show *Girlfriends,* it was the episode where Joan and William were trying to make up a Cinco DeMaio dance routine. I almost peed on myself, no matter how many times I saw these damn episodes I was always weak. I made it to the bathroom just in time before I had an accident and I heard my phone ring from a distance. I sat on the toilet for an extra five minutes just because my big self couldn't get up. I was damn near five months, but was big as hell, all stomach.

My phone rang aging when I made it back to the bed and it was my aunt Pat. I started not to answer, but I knew that she would only call again.

"Hey Aunt Pat," I answered. Immediately I could tell that she was crying.

"Baby, Pisces is in a mental a hospital. She done gone crazy and attacked me," she was somewhat inaudible from all the sobbing that she was doing.

"What hospital? I'm on my way there," I said as I slipped on pants and Ugg slides and grabbed my crutches.

After getting the address, I made my way to the hospital worried to death. P was a lot of things but disrespectful to her mom was never her. I met my aunty in the waiting room, and she was still crying.

"Baby what happened to you?" she asked pointing to the crutches that I was sporting.

"Nothing, aunty. What happened with P?"

"Oh Mocha, I didn't know what to do. She lunged at me with a knife. I had to call the police."

"It will be okay. Where is she now?" I asked.

"I think they sedated her, but she's right back here," she led me to a back room.

P was laying in the bed with her eyes half open and her hair all over her head. There was dried up saliva around her mouth and her stomach was now deflated.

"Aunty did she have the baby?" I asked. Pat then began to cry again, and I went to comfort her.

"Did she lose the baby?"

"Uhhh huh! She did months ago, but it was a still born. Pisces never even came to the hospital. A dead baby was in her stomach for a while now. The doctors couldn't tell when the baby died but it has been two months or more and they did a C-section to take the baby out."

She sobbed on my shoulder and I was so disturbed. P had really lost it to have a dead baby inside of her for so long. I wondered if it was the death of Zoe or what. P wouldn't even look at me. She just laid there still; her eyes fixated on nothing at all. There was no life in her eyes at all. The old lively P was not there, and some alien had replaced that girl. I felt myself on the verge of crying and I knew it was my damn pregnant hormones.

I hopped out of the room, no longer able to contain myself. I cried and cried in my car thinking of the man changes that had happened in my life in the last few months. Shit was just not the same.

LA

I watched Mocha as she limped into the house. It was 11pm and I guess she just said fuck the crutches. Baby girl wore a frown on her face, and I could tell she had been crying from the red puffy rings around her eyes. I wanted so badly to console her, but I knew that she would only push me away. She shouldn't have to be alone during her pregnancy, but she didn't even know that I was around more than she thought. I kissed her every morning before she woke up and every night before she went to bed. I would always be around to protect her.

After I made sure that Mo was straight, I made my way to my mama crib to borrow her couch. My new location was too far of a drive, so I would thug it out with her for the night. When I walked in, I expected her to be out like at light, but I heard running water in the kitchen.

"Mama! Hell, you doin-"

My words were caught in my throat when I saw my mom laying on the floor clutching her chest. I picked her up and carried her my car and sped through the night to the hospital. My heart was beating so damn fast that I could hardly breathe. I didn't know what I would do if I lost my mam. She was only sixty-two years old and as healthy as an ox.

Ashlyn met me at the hospital when a sleeping Ross on her hip. Ross somehow made me feel just a little bit lighter. I hugged her tightly causing her to wake up.

"Uncle La, what's wrong?' I guess she noticed my vibe.

"Nana's a little sick, but I will be okay."

"Where is she? Can I see her?" she asked innocently.

"Not right now baby," Ashlyn cut in. "Nana needs her rest and you will see her later," Ashlyn lied. Mama had suffered a heart attack and was in surgery as we spoke. I sat there holding Ross tight as she fell asleep in my arms an before we knew, it was morning and I was being awaken by a doctor.

Ashlyn wiped the cold out of her eyes and grabbed hold of my hand. I drifted into another universe as I heard the doctor say those fatal words. My mother would no longer be able to rag on me about settling down. She would never be able to cook me those good ole southern meals and most of all she would be leaving her baby boy behind. I was officially alone. Both of my brothers were gone, Zoe and now my mama. I had nothing to live for.

MOCHA

I rang LA's phone about six times before finally giving up. It was the day that I would be finding out what I would be having. We hadn't been talking, but I did want him to come along to this appointment. He deserved to know anything that included his child and I would grant him that. Too bad his ass wasn't answering the phone, so I called Ashlyn, but she didn't answer either. The two of them were pissing me off so I just went to my appointment alone. I cried tears of joy finding out that I was indeed having a baby boy. I would kick Ashlyn and LA's asses for making me have a damn boy, but I was a little bummed out that he wasn't her to witness it. LA had taught me more than he thought, He thought that I didn't know that he would stalk my house and shit at night, but I knew. He always taught me to be aware or my surroundings and watch my back at all times and I did.

"When I left the doctors, Ashtyn finally answered the phone, "Well damn hoe, about time!" I started.

"Mocha."

"Girl don't Mocha me!"

"Mocha shut the fuck up damn and let me talk. LA's mom passed away this morning. We been at the hospital all night."

Silence

I didn't even know what to say. Lately, people were dropping like flies in LA's life. I needed to call him to see how he was doing. "Oh my god Ash, how is LA doing?"

"Girl you know he strong as an ox, but he really hurting. But anyway, I going to start getting these burial plans and I will talk to you later."

"Okay sis, call me if you need help with anything." The call ended.

I sat in my car with my hand on my belly. I could never imagine losing someone so close to me and I didn't know what to say to comfort LA, but I would be there for him no matter if we were together or not. I dialed up his number, but it went to the voice mail after the first ring. I tried back calling again and got the same response. I even rode pass his house and sat outside for a few, but he never came home.

My mind automatically went to the worst as I hoped that he wouldn't do anything to harm himself. I instantly dropped to my knees and prayed that he would make it through this difficult time. I prayed that he found his strength and that this was the wakeup call that he needed.

LA

Thanks to Ash, everything for my mom's funeral was handled in a timely manner. Exactly six days after my mom was taken from this earth, she was laid to rest in nothing but the finest. Her funeral was held at The Mount Baptist church and over two hundred people attended. There was not a dry eye in the house, but for some reason I couldn't shed a tear. I felt like I had to remain stoic or else the streets would sleep on me. My heart hurt so badly and that hurt in turn was anger. I didn't have any kickin' it for anyone family or not.

People was coming up to me offering condolences and shit, but I could piss on their condolences. My two brothers and my mom were gone and that was some shit that I would never heal from. I was not one to sit around and laugh with folks after a funeral, so I grabbed me a few bottles and got low. Mocha had been blowing my sit up, but I didn't want to talk to her ass either. She gave up on me when I needed her, so she was dead to me too.

I didn't want to do anything other than what I was doing right now and that was getting high and drunk. I called out to my mama, but she wasn't there and that hurt me to the core. How could I call on her and she not answer? The bottle crashing against the window pane maddened me even more as the first tear fell from my eyes. My family was gone.

I must've have fell asleep because I was awakened by the incessant hammering at my door. I looked out of the window to see Mocha and Ashlyn, two people that I did not want to see. Hell, I didn't want to see anyone so they would remain outside. The two knocked for about twenty minutes before they finally gave up. I wasn't a sucker like Mo, who hid a spare key under the door mat.

I wondered if this is what depression feels like. I had no desire to interact with the outside world and nothing made me happy, not even the thought of my unborn. I had only been depressed like this one time before and that is when Roscoe died. My body count got higher and my patience grew thinner. I didn't want to go back to that person, but it seemed like I would have no choice.

MOCHA

I hadn't spoken to LA in weeks and he ignored me at his mother's funeral. Since then I had been calling him and stopping by his house, but he only hid. He wasn't even talking to Ross and Ashlyn which was very odd. He loved his niece with everything in him, so I knew that he was hurting. I got up from the bed as it seemed like my stomach weighed more than me. I was going on seven months and yes time was flying. It seemed like just yesterday when I was found out the sex. A this point, this little boy was about to get its eviction notice. I walked to baby Liam's room and it was almost finished. He had a crib, changing table, rocking chair, booster seat and more. Now I just need to paint the walls. I was thinking of Periwinkle Blue.

It was almost eight pm and I needed to start getting things for Ross. Ashlyn was going out on a date with Slim tonight finally and I volunteered to babysit. I wouldn't give her any reason to say that she couldn't go. I looked in the fridge and it was just as empty, so I decided to go pick up a few things from the market. I shopped for about forty five minute before leaving, but ultimately being sucked into getting ice-cream by my kicking baby. As I walked to the store my mouth watered at the thought of cookie dough ice-cream mixed with mouse tracks. My boys favorite.

I got an entire tub and decided to eat in it walking to the car, when I heard the faint sounds of a child. I stopped munching on my ice cream and looked toward the back alley and indeed there was a child who looked like he was hurt. I cautiously walked over to him and he was holding his stomach groaning, but he couldn't have been any older than ten or eleven. "Honey, are you okay?" I asked. "Where are your parents?"

"Uhhh," he whined. "I ran and fell," his voice sounded a little too deep to be a pre-teen.

I walked closer to him and as he lifted his shirt a gun appeared. A worried expression crossed my face while a smiled now covered his. I grabbed my stomach and started to slowly walk backwards, and the boy aimed the gun at me.

"One thing before you go, miss. Tell yo' bitch ass nigga we even and this is for Lou!" In one swift motion his finger hit the trigger and I felt one bullet after another enter my body. I fell back and immediately felt cold. I guess this is what death felt like, but I had been shot before so this couldn't have been the end for me.

It turns out that that kid that I wanted to help in a dark alley was actually a man with a birth defect that altered his developmental growth. As I laid there on that cold ground I wondered if LA would have the strength to come to my funeral or if he knew that I loved him from the moment that I had saw him and I still did. My thoughts then went to my Baby boy who would never experience the joy of life all because his mama couldn't finish eating her ice-cream and mind her business. I just hoped that my baby and LA forgave me.

LA

THREE MONTHS LATER

The sun shinned brightly as the family of birds flew over my head flocked to a tree. They looked like a little happy family. The mama bird hawked over the baby birds and the father bird watched protectively from a distance. The sight or anything or anyone being happy or normally functioning got to me sometimes since I no longer had my mother in my life. I was finding better ways of coping now as I learned that the answer to my problems were not going to be found at the bottom of any bottle.

I neared my destination and my anxiety was on ten. Every time that It was time to see my family I choked up. I didn't even know why, but I hadn't been to see them since they had been buried. There were all in a burial plot together. Mom in the middle and both of her sons alongside of her with my dad at the far end.

"Hey mama. I know I know I haven't been out here to see you in a while, but I was really hurting. Losing you was not easy, but I promise I won't stay away this long ever again." I looked back and forth at my two brothers. "CJ and Sco, ya'll better be looking out for me up there. Ya'll niggas always been goofy as hell anyway, probably up there or where ever y'all are joking and clowning," I started to chuckle at all the dumb sit that we used to do. "I miss ya'll like hell though!" I touched Sco's grave and my hand stayed there for a while.

I looked over on the other side of the plot and there sat alone headstone with man flowers around it. My first tear fell as I walked over and said Hi to my baby girl. Mocha's family was nice enough to let me have her buried in my family's plot. They had even relocated to Philly so that they could be closer to us. Seeing Mo was the hardest because she was the love of my life. At first, I cursed her name for making such a mistake and leaving me, and then I blamed myself for ignoring her and not being there to protect her like I had promised, but then I realized that I couldn't sit and dwell on something that I couldn't change. Yes, I missed her like hell and probably would never recover from this heartache, but I had to get myself together.

That night that I saw her in that Alley covered with a white sheet, my immediate thought was to paint the town red going after any and everybody, but the situation kind of handled itself. King Louie killed Sherman because he was getting high as a rocket stealing his supply and the lil' nigga that they called baby managed to get himself in a car accident two weeks after he kill Mocha.

I sat in front of her grave and only stared. I tried to remember her corny jokes that she used to tell or that passionate look in her eyes when she did what she loved most and that was help people. I didn't think I would ever give my heart fully to any chick, but she came along and changed my mind. It killed me inside to know that she was taken from this earth because of some bullshit that involved me. My girl was gone because of me.

"Nigga get yo' ass up off of that ground. My sister don't like all of the crying shit." I heard a voice say from behind me. I grabbed my waist, but my frown was immediately turned upside down as Yahseem walked up.

"Man, don't you see I'm trying to have some alone time with my girl. I keep telling you she done booted your ass out the way," I joked dapping him up

Yahseem and I had come a long way as we went from being enemies on different sides to connected by a tragic event. I looked down at the car seat that he was holding, and I beamed. There was my little man knocked out like he had a hard day at work. Mocha had been hit five times and ultimately died in surgery, but the doctors were able to save my boy. Due to him being born early he was in the hospital for the first two months and when he was well and strong enough, they let him come home. Now my son was doing better than ever, and I was just glad that I had someone who made me just a little closer with Mocha.

I scooped him up in my arms and a little smile appeared on his face. I guess he was dreaming of angels like the old folks used to say.

"So how long you gone be up here bruh?" Yahseem asked me.

"Man, I don't even know. I just want some time with my peeps and thanks for picking up Liam."

"It ain't no thang, but I'ma get on up out of here. You know grave yard freak me out, but keep you head up." Yahseem dapped me up once more before touching Mocha's head stone and leaving. It took Yah and me a while before we even started talking. We legit hated each other and he blamed me for Mochas death at first. I didn't even know that he had escaped from some shit that King Lou had got him in, but he said that, that situation alone told him that if was time to leave the game. I guess that's how we bonded, because we were on the same page with the gang shit. Mocha had already told me that I had lost more battles than I had won, and those words were finally starting to set in for me.

So now, Yah and I were no longer members of NHG and NBK. I got some backlash for it at first, but that shit didn't matter. I had a little man to think about now and nothing that the niggas was saying ever moved me. No one had seen or heard from Peaches and I just figured that she was up under some nigga with some money, and as for Pisces, she was still in the crazy hospital calling out her dead baby's name.

My phone rang and it was Ashlyn's ass, my sister and I were closer than ever, but her ass was still worrisome calling me all day to check on Liam. Ash was now dating Slim and though it bothered me at first, but the nigga was no longer with NBK so I didn't fuss much. Ash seemed genuinely happy and my niece liked him so that is all that I cared about. And let's not get started on Ross, she really thought that Liam was her baby. She wanted to spend every weekend with me just to play mommy to him and I loved it, they asses was gone be close as ever. Now and days I

TESHERA C.

valued family more than ever, so I had to keep my people close to me. I had my son, my sister, niece and a newfound friend so now I had everything to live for.

THE END

NOTE FROM THE AUTHOR

BumbleTee's, stayed tuned. This is a standalone, but you may hear from LA, War, and Chaotic again in the future. Also, be sure to leave a review on Amazon, good or bad I would love your feedback. Book five will be here before you know it.

ABOUT THE AUTHOR

Teshera Cooper is a 27-year-old new author who hails from Norfolk, Virginia. She has a bachelor's degree in psychology from Old Dominion University. While she has a passion for mental health and advocates for black excellence that has never stopped her from turning the vivid imagery that consumes her thoughts into short stories. She has been writing short stories since about 14 years old and drew inspiration from her upbringing and from her experiences from growing up in the "hood". Each of the characters that she creates embodies someone that she has encountered; from the dope boys on the street corner to the hot in the pants girl who deep down inside just wants to be loved.

Teshera is devoted to giving her readers a fast paced and gritty thrill ride with a twist of hood love. Writers who have inspired her include, Terri woods, Sista Soulja, Carl Webber, Wahida Clark, Vickie Stranger, K'wan, Ashley & Jaquavis and countless others. The way that they can bring life into their characters with just the stroke of a pen is pure genius and that is what she aspires to do through her writing.

facebook.com/TeelaMarieCooper

instagram.com/Teela_marie18

Royalty Publishing House is now accepting manuscripts from aspiring or experienced urban romance authors!

WHAT MAY PLACE YOU ABOVE THE REST:

Heroes who are the ultimate book bae: strong-willed, maybe a little rough around the edges but willing to risk it all for the woman he loves.

Heroines who are the ultimate match: the girl next door type, not perfect - has her faults but is still a decent person. One who is willing to risk it all for the man she loves.

The rest is up to you! Just be creative, think out of the box, keep it sexy and intriguing!

If you'd like to join the Royal family, send us the first 15K words (60 pages) of your completed manuscript to submissions@royaltypublishing-house.com

LIKE OUR PAGE!

Be sure to LIKE our Royalty Publishing House page on Facebook!